The second armed Jeep swept into view

The man behind the machine gun hadn't known what to expect, but it most certainly wasn't to have a friendly gun turned on him. Bolan raked the Jeep from front to back, bullets punching into the hood and windshield. The driver jerked back, his chest and head pulverized by the continuous blast of automatic fire.

The Jeep swerved and ran on for yards b̶̶̶ the engine stalled and it rattled to a s̶̶̶ Executioner hammered at it until̶̶̶ contents caught a spark and e̶̶̶ surge of flame.

The surviving traffickers̶̶̶ themselves together for a c̶̶̶ Bolan's vehicle, but the Executioner ̶̶̶ barrel of his weapon back on line and̶̶̶ted more damage. Under his relentless fire, the men went down hard, bodies bloodied and torn.

Bolan's finger released the trigger and the chatter of the machine gun ceased. All that remained was the moaning of the wounded. The dead held their peace.

The Executioner knew the clock was ticking. Though the numbers were still falling, he knew without a shadow of doubt there would be others.

How long he might hold them back was anyone's guess.

MACK BOLAN ®

The Executioner

The Executioner

Don Pendleton's ®

CARTEL CLASH

A GOLD EAGLE BOOK FROM

W✺RLDWIDE ®

TORONTO • NEW YORK • LONDON
AMSTERDAM • PARIS • SYDNEY • HAMBURG
STOCKHOLM • ATHENS • TOKYO • MILAN
MADRID • WARSAW • BUDAPEST • AUCKLAND

Recycling programs
for this product may
not exist in your area.

First edition November 2010

ISBN-13: 978-0-373-64384-4

Special thanks and acknowledgment to
Mike Linaker for his contribution to this work.

CARTEL CLASH

Printed in U.S.A.

May God have mercy upon my enemies, because I sure as hell won't.

—George S. Patton
1885–1945

No matter how long and bloody the conflict, the drug war has to be faced head-on. Those engaged in the trafficking of narcotics have no scruples. No conscience. Their victims do not concern these people. All they see are the dollars their foul product earns. If we are to engage, our resolve has to be unshakable and our tactics as ruthless as theirs.

—Mack Bolan

THE
MACK BOLAN

LEGEND

Nothing less than a war could have fashioned the destiny of the man called Mack Bolan. Bolan earned the Executioner title in the jungle hell of Vietnam.

But this soldier also wore another name—Sergeant Mercy. He was so tagged because of the compassion he showed to wounded comrades-in-arms and Vietnamese civilians.

Mack Bolan's second tour of duty ended prematurely when he was given emergency leave to return home and bury his family, victims of the Mob. Then he declared a one-man war against the Mafia.

He confronted the Families head-on from coast to coast, and soon a hope of victory began to appear. But Bolan had broken society's every rule. That same society started gunning for this elusive warrior—to no avail.

So Bolan was offered amnesty to work within the system against terrorism. This time, as an employee of Uncle Sam, Bolan became Colonel John Phoenix. With a command center at Stony Man Farm in Virginia, he and his new allies—Able Team and Phoenix Force—waged relentless war on a new adversary: the KGB.

But when his one true love, April Rose, died at the hands of the Soviet terror machine, Bolan severed all ties with Establishment authority.

Now, after a lengthy lone-wolf struggle and much soul-searching, the Executioner has agreed to enter an "arm's-length" alliance with his government once more, reserving the right to pursue personal missions in his Everlasting War.

Prologue

Border Country, Texas

"It never ceases to amaze me," Preacher said, "how ingenious folk can be when it comes to making things that do harm."

He was fingering a strand of the razor wire that stretched across the tract of land where Texas met Mexico. It ran in an unbroken line east to west, a man-made barrier cutting across the invisible border.

Choirboy, his partner, nodded in agreement, shifting his gaze to the barely moving figure spread-eagled across the wire. The man's earlier struggles had slowed imperceptibly until he was almost motionless. His initial twisting and turning had caused countless cuts and gashes in his naked flesh, and he was torn and bloody.

"No question it ain't doin' him any favors," he said.

Preacher shaded his eyes as he glanced skyward. The sun was directly overhead. Hot and bright. The man on the wire was unprotected and unable to save himself from what was to come. Preacher didn't figure on more than a couple of hours.

"Let's get the hell out of here," he said. "Something cool in a long glass is my choice."

They turned and walked to the 4x4 parked close by. Choirboy drove, turning the vehicle in the direction of the dirt road roughly two miles away. From there a twenty-minute ride would bring them to the main highway.

Preacher took out his cell phone and hit speed dial. He listened as the number rang out. When it was answered, he recognized the voice immediately.

"She's done," Preacher said.

"Fine. The rest of your fee will be transferred by morning."

"Hell, I wasn't calling about that. Just to let you know the problem has been resolved."

"Okay."

The call over, Preacher put away his phone and turned on the radio. The station was local, playing some country and western.

"Now that is nice," Choirboy said.

"It is so, too," Preacher said. "Push that pedal down, son, I'm getting real thirsty."

THE MAN LEFT BEHIND on the razor wire took another hour to die. The savage beating he had received before being thrown on the barrier had weakened him already. He had two broken arms, broken ribs and a bad fracture in his left leg. The deep wounds inflicted by the steel razor barbs had accelerated his loss of blood, and the dehydrating and burning effect of the overhead sun hastened his death.

It was another full day before the body was discovered by a border patrol team. Hardened though they might have been by the things they had witnessed, the two-man team was shocked at the brutality of the violence that had led to the man's death. A department chopper was called in, and after the body had been recovered it was flown to the closest medical center where an autopsy was carried out and the task of identifying the dead man was initiated.

It took only a couple of hours for fingerprint and dental ID to confirm who the man was: Don Manners, a six-year veteran of the DEA. During the six months preceding his murder, Manners had been operating undercover, working his way into the drug cartel headed by Benito Rojas and his American partner,

Marshal Dembrow. Three days earlier Manners had managed to communicate with his superiors about an incoming arms shipment to the Rojas Cartel. Although he had not managed to pass on the finer details, Manners had reported that, along with conventional weapons, Rojas had negotiated the purchase of a couple of mobile, high-end missile units. There was nothing in Manners's report that told when and where the consignment was due, but he spoke of a Russian supplier.

The DEA, despite this intel, was still helpless. If the ordnance was coming into Mexico, it was out of their jurisdiction, and they could do nothing except stand by and imagine Rojas taking great pleasure in his latest move against the U.S. authorities.

The report, in full, found its way to Washington, and eventually to the desk of the American President because he had asked to be kept in the loop with anything to do with the drug trade. It held great interest for the President. It was a cause, among many others, that stirred his emotions. Since coming into office, he had made the eradication of the drug tide a priority. Despite his efforts and the responses of the DEA, little headway had been made. The President was far from happy. His hands, though, were tied. The particular items that fueled his mood this time were the savage slaughter of Don Manners and the revelation that Rojas was importing missiles—missiles he'd undoubtedly use in his declared war against the Americans who had destroyed a great deal of his merchandise. Rojas's response had been to increase the amount of drugs he shipped over the border, while also escalating his unremitting violence against anyone who defied him.

The President had read and reread the report, sitting alone in the Oval Office, his frustration over the situation growing with each passing minute. He hated the thought of more drugs coming into the country, the misery it would cause, and the cruel indifference of men like Rojas and Dembrow. They were defying the might of the U.S., killing at will, and ignoring every law and rule in the book. All the while becoming richer day by day.

It had to stop.

The President reached for the phone on his desk that would

connect him with the one man who might be able to assist in resolving the situation.

The phone rang out and was quickly picked up.

"Mr. President."

"We need to talk, Hal. ASAP. There's something I need your help with."

Mack Bolan spotted the young woman as she came down the wooden stairs tacked on to the side of the cantina. The stairs led to the two-roomed apartment Don Manners had been using during his time in Texas. The location had come from the file Brognola had given Bolan when he'd accepted the assignment. The file had updated the Executioner on the local situation, and it made frustrating reading. Drug enforcement agencies, well versed in the illegal activities, were stifled because the Rojas Cartel and its Texas chapter, though they didn't have right, they certainly had might on their side. It was an all too familiar story. The drug organizations were ultimately so powerful they defied any and all attempts at taking them down. The endless wealth they generated from their trade allowed them to buy legal help of the highest order. If any of their people were arrested, the ink was not even dry on the paperwork before lawyers were hammering on the police station doors. Witnesses were either bought off or wiped out. The indifference to law and order was staggering. The authorities understood the situation that forced them to stand off, watching in jurisdictional paralysis while the enemy went about its business with impunity. The busts they did manage to make stick were small victories and something the drug cartels could well afford.

The Manners murder was a direct slap in the face of the DEA task force. An open statement from the drug world.

We can do this because you can't pin it on us. You have nothing on us. Send in your agents, and we will return them all in a similar way.

The file Brognola had given Bolan during their briefing on the upcoming mission had contained images of Manners—where he had been found and what had been done to him.

"Enough is enough," Brognola had said. "The President has taken this on board because he's had it with these sick bastards, Striker. The head of the most powerful nation on Earth and he's helpless, because he can't do a damn thing legally."

Bolan had smiled at the last word—legally—and he understood exactly what was coming next.

"The President, me and you, Striker. We're the only ones in the loop on this one. He's asking for your help. The kind of help only you can provide. Nothing on the books. Nothing that connects this mission to him, or the U.S. administration. I'll provide any logistical assistance you need through Stony Man. No questions asked as to how, or where, or when. He just wants Rojas and Dembrow gone. Their business wiped out. And this incoming special cargo, as well."

Brognola had waited as Bolan scanned the file. The Executioner was as committed to doing whatever possible to inflict damage on the purveyors of illegal drug trafficking as anyone, and the fact the President was asking for his covert assistance alerted him to the gravity of the situation.

"Well?" Brognola asked after a decent interval.

"I get triple brownie points?" Bolan asked archly.

Brognola only hesitated for effect. "Hell of a request, but okay."

BOLAN IMMEDIATELY MADE his way to the small Texas town close to the border to make his first contact.

The young woman, dark-haired, slim and pretty, from what Bolan could see, clutched a small cloth bundle, and her cautious manner told Bolan she should not have been in the apartment. His curiosity was aroused. The young woman was his first possible lead to Manners. At the moment he had no idea how important her relationship with the agent might have been, but he had to find out.

His rented Ford 4x4 was parked across the street from the cantina. Bolan watched as his lead walked quickly by the frontage. As Bolan leaned forward to fire up the engine, he saw two figures detach from the shadows of the alley beside the cantina and fall in behind the young woman. It looked as if others were interested in her, too.

Beyond the cantina were a couple of closed and shuttered stores, then an empty lot covered with weeds and refuse. Bolan eased open the truck's door and stepped out. He crossed the street and trailed the pair following the woman. The men remained at a discreet distance until she turned to cross the empty lot, then they upped their pace. Bolan did the same, his long legs covering the distance with ease. As he rounded the end of the last store, he saw the duo closing in on their mark, heard her startled gasp as one of them reached out to catch hold of one of her arms and jerk her to a stop. One of the men spoke, his Spanish so rapid that Bolan only caught a few words. Understandable or not, the menace in the guy's tone was unmistakable. The woman replied, her words defiant.

"*Puta,*" the man yelled, and slapped her across the face. The blow knocked the woman off her feet. "*Puta madre.*"

The second man leaned down to snatch at the bundle from her arms. She yelled at him, clinging to the package. The guy kicked at her side.

That was when Bolan reached the group. He went for the guy who had kicked the young woman, grabbed a handful of his thick black hair and yanked hard. The man yelled, trying to turn. Bolan slammed a hard fist into the goon's exposed ribs. He put all of his strength into the blow and heard the faint crack of bone. The man groaned. The Executioner drove the toe of his boot into the back of one knee. The leg buckled, the man losing balance, and as his opponent fell backward the soldier snapped an arm around his lean neck and dragged him close. He stamped down on the man's calf, breaking the limb. The man screamed as Bolan let go and swiveled to face the first guy, who had produced a knife from his belt. He lunged wildly at his adversary, and from the way he moved it was obvious he was no expert.

"Bastardo."

The knife had a thick, heavy blade and it slowed the guy's desperate slashes. Even so, Bolan kept his eye on the weaving length of steel. He was an experienced knife fighter, and even the clumsiest attacker only had to get lucky once.

Bolan avoided the first couple of uncoordinated thrusts, watching the blade as it completed its arc. In the moment it swung at him again, Bolan stepped in, caught the knife arm, turned his body into his opponent's space and used his free arm to hammer the point of his elbow into the man's face. The blow was delivered without hesitation and with crippling force. The knife man's cry of pain was reduced to a choking gurgle as blood from his crushed nose and shattered teeth filled his mouth. When Bolan added pressure, the knife slipped from limp fingers. The soldier reached back and gripped a handful of the guy's shirt. He yanked forward, bending so that his adversary was pulled over his shoulder. The man slammed onto the hard ground with a solid thud, with Bolan standing over him. He never saw the heavy swing of the Executioner's boot. It connected with the back of his skull and slammed him into oblivion.

A warning yell from the dark-haired woman drew Bolan's attention. He turned and saw the first guy reach for something tucked into his belt. He saw the dark outline of an autopistol rise. Stepping to the man's blind side, Bolan delivered a brutal kick to his head. The hard impact drove him facedown on the dusty ground. Leaning over, the soldier picked up the pistol and jammed it beneath his own belt, under the black leather jacket he was wearing. He checked their pockets but found little except tight rolls of paper money. Bolan took them. Cash was sometimes a handy way of smoothing over complications.

Then he bent over the slim form of the woman, gently grasping a bare arm. She resisted, still dazed from the attack, but there was not a lot of fight left in her.

"I'm not going to hurt you," Bolan said. "Just want to get you away from here. *¿Entiendes?*"

She looked up at him, brushing black hair away from her pale face. A thin line of blood seeped from the corner of her soft mouth.

"Yes, I understand English."

"Good," Bolan said, "because my Spanish isn't always that clear."

He helped her to her feet. She swayed a little, then steadied herself. She still clutched the bundle to her.

"Let's go," Bolan said.

She hesitated, her eyes wide and cautious.

"Go where?"

"Somewhere away from these people."

She stared at him for long seconds, and Bolan sensed her mind was whirling with thoughts. He understood her suspicions.

"You were a friend of Don Manners?" A quick nod. "Then we're on the same side. Now let's get the hell out of here in case those two have backup."

He took her slim hand in his and led her back toward the street, across to where his 4x4 was parked. Bolan saw her into the passenger seat, then climbed behind the wheel and fired up the engine. He eased along the street, heading for the center of town where there were more people, light and his motel.

The young woman had slumped back in the seat, her face turned away from view, hugging the bundle she carried. The way she held on to it was working on Bolan's curiosity. He didn't ask her about it. There was time for that once he had her off the street.

It was close to eleven p.m. The town's main drag was crowded. The street was busy with traffic, so it took Bolan a while to reach the turn for the motel. He eased through the pedestrians, cleared the town. It was quieter here, the street almost deserted. The motel was a half mile along the strip of road. Bolan drove into the courtyard through the adobe arch, angling the truck to a stop outside his room. He cut the engine and stepped out, then circled the vehicle to open the passenger door.

"Best room in the house," he said. "I promise."

The woman climbed out. Bolan guided her to the door and unlocked it. He pushed the door open and stood back to let her go inside. She stood in the center of the room, staring at her surroundings. Bolan quietly closed and locked the door. He shuttered the window blind and put on the main light, leaving her alone while he went into the bathroom and ran warm water in the basin. He chose a small towel and soaked half of it in the water, squeezing out the excess. When he got back in the main room, the woman was sitting on the end of the bed.

"For your face," Bolan said, holding out the towel.

She took it and held it against her mouth. Bolan noticed she had placed her mysterious package on the bed next to her. He ignored it, crossing to the armchair facing the bed. He sat, giving her time to tend to her injury. A bruise was forming on her lower cheek, discoloring her tawny complexion.

In the room light he could see she was attractive, her face dominated by large brown eyes and softly plump lips. Her shoulder-length black hair was thick and shiny. Beneath the soft cotton shirt and faded jeans, her figure was lithe and feminine.

"I'm Matt Cooper," he said.

"You are a friend of Don?"

"We never met."

"But you said…" Her eyes sought the door, her body tensing.

"I said I was on the same side. I came to find out what happened to him."

"He was killed."

"And why do you think that happened?"

"If you knew who he was, then you should know why Don was here."

"He told you?"

"He told me many things." Her face crumpled as she failed to hold in her feelings. "He was going to take me with him when he was finished here."

"It was like that?"

She nodded, drew in a breath and regained control.

"We didn't seek what happened. It just did...."

"Were you helping Don?

"A little, *sí*."

"Against Benito Rojas?"

"*Sí*. Against Rojas and Dembrow."

"Tell me who you are."

"Pilar Trujillo."

"I told you I came here to find out how Don died. That's only part of the reason. I'm also here to put a stop to Rojas's business." Bolan saw the sudden gleam in her eyes. "You understand that?"

"Yes. Rojas trades in drugs. And other things. But mainly in drugs. I know that is why Don was here. To gather information for the DEA. He had found out Rojas was waiting for an important cargo. Some new weapon he will use to fight the Americans. It was this information that got him killed. He made a slip, and it exposed who he was—an American DEA undercover agent." Pilar fell silent. Her eyes mirrored the torment she was struggling to contain. She stared directly at Bolan. "Don was exposed and betrayed. That is why they did what they did to him. To show the Americans you cannot stand against the Rojas Cartel."

"Pilar, do you know how it happened? Who betrayed Don?"

Pilar's eyes brimmed with tears. "*Sí*, I know. It was one of Rojas's lieutenants. His name is Tomas. Tomas Trujillo. He is my brother."

2

"Your brother works for Rojas?"

"He works for the Rojas Cartel, which also includes Marshal Dembrow. It is something I am not proud of. If our parents were still alive, they would disown him. Tomas is now the head of the family."

"What about the pair who attacked you?"

"They are Mexicans who are part of Dembrow's crew. They have been following me for some days, watching me because they believed I had more information Don left behind. I think they were waiting to see if I went to get it. Tomas has gone back to Mexico, to Rojas's ranch. Since Don's death, Rojas is suspicious of everyone. Even Dembrow."

Bolan filed that away. It was an interesting development, maybe something he could play on to give himself some leverage.

"So, do you?" he asked, picking up on Pilar's earlier remark.

"What?"

"You said Dembrow's men believed you had information Manners left behind."

"*Sí,*" she said.

Bolan pointed at the bundle on the bed. "In there?"

"No. That was simply a distraction. I hoped they would snatch it from me and run. Give me time to get away. Foolish, maybe, but it was all I could think of at the time."

She unrolled the bundle and showed Bolan the contents, which were personal items from Manners's room.

"This is what they should have been looking for," Pilar said, sliding her hand from a pocket of her jeans and showing a much-used silver flint lighter.

Bolan took it from her. Turning it over in his hand he slid the outer casing from the lighter. The wad of absorbent material came free when he tugged at it. Bolan pulled it apart and found a thin, tight roll of clear plastic. He unrolled it and extracted a narrow strip of paper. The strip held a single line of neat writing—figures, and a name. The figures looked like a telephone number: a country code, followed by a local code and the number itself. The name on the paper was Calderon.

"Don told me if anything happened I was to get the lighter and pass it on to his people in El Paso. He had not been able to transmit this last piece of evidence."

"No other information?"

"Nothing. Do you believe it will help?"

"Maybe."

Bolan walked over to the other side of the room and took out his sat phone and hit the speed dial for his connection to Stony Man.

"I need a rundown on a possible phone number and a name," he said when Barbara Price, Stony Man's mission controller, picked up. He read off the number and the name. "Get back to me ASAP."

"Will do. How's it going?"

"Interesting," Bolan said. And with that he ended the call.

Pilar was watching him closely as he put the phone away.

"I do not suppose it would do me any good to ask who you were talking to?"

Bolan smiled. "No good at all. But I have an idea. There's a diner just along the road. How about we go get coffee and something to eat. I haven't had a thing since breakfast."

Pilar, realizing she was not about to gain any further knowledge, nodded. "Just let me use the bathroom," she said. "I need to freshen up."

Finally alone, Bolan checked out the handgun he had acquired. It was a 9 mm SIG-Sauer P-226, holding a 15-round magazine. His own ordnance was still in a carry-all, secured in the motel room's closet. The P-226 would serve his needs for the present and conserve his own supply of ammunition. He slid out the clip and saw it was full. Replacing it, he worked the first round into the breech and put the pistol behind his belt, under his shirt.

"Hey, it's only a diner we're going to," Pilar said, exiting the bathroom.

"Well, going by some diners I've visited, a gun might come in handy," Bolan said lightly.

He saw her smile, albeit briefly.

They left the room and walked away from the motel. The diner, on the same side of the wide street, was a few hundred yards away. The place was empty of customers. Bolan chose a booth at the far end of the room that allowed them a clear view of the interior and the door.

Pilar watched Bolan's actions, and it occurred to her that he was just like Manners—cautious and taking in everything around him, but maintaining an outward facade of calm. Whomever this man was, he struck her as being professional and capable of handling himself. She recalled the swift, efficient way he had dealt with Dembrow's men. Watching him now, his easy way with the server, she might have been in the company of a totally different man.

"Coffee?" he asked, and it took a couple of seconds before she registered.

Pilar nodded and found herself responding without thinking. *"Sí."*

Bolan had observed the way she had slumped against the seat, shoulders down, and he realized she was reacting to what had happened. The unprovoked attack had left its mark and now she was struggling to come to terms with it. He quietly ordered food for both of them. When they were alone again, he saw Pilar's slim hands on the table. They were trembling visibly. Bolan reached out and placed his big hands over hers, squeezing gently, holding them until the trembling faded. "It's been a tough night," he said softly, his voice gentle. "Come morning, I'll do my best to get you away from here."

Her soft brown eyes sought his. She stared at him and looked hard into the startling blue and she saw that he meant what he had said.

"*Gracias*. What about you? You must understand how terrible these people are," she said.

"I know all about Marshal Dembrow and Benito Rojas. It's why I came here. Believe me, Pilar, their time is coming."

"For that alone I thank you."

Their coffee arrived, and while they waited for the food to come Bolan picked up their conversation.

"Let's talk about Dembrow. What's the situation here? Does Dembrow have local influence?"

"That was why Don came. His orders were to get inside Dembrow's organization and collect as much information as he could. He did. At first his mission appeared to be going well. He was very clever at making friends. While he did that he watched and listened, picking up things here and there. Even Dembrow began to like him. Don understood how men like Dembrow worked. With all the drug money coming in, Dembrow was able to buy protection beyond his own people."

"Police? Border Patrol?"

Pilar nodded. "Don suspected some officials of being on Dembrow's payroll, those who looked the other way when he ran an operation. It's why the cartel is able to get their drugs across the border in such quantities." She brushed stray hair back from her face as she collected her thoughts. "The Rojas Cartel is extremely powerful, but I suppose you know this already. The money they make has given them the ability to become so arrogant they believe they can ignore the law and do what they want. No one dare stand against them. Any who have in the past end up dead in ditches. Or have accidents. Rojas and Dembrow simply give the order, hand over the money and problems disappear. They are above the law."

"It looks to me," Bolan said, "that a change is in order."

Food was brought to the table and placed in front of them. Bolan had ordered steaks with all the trimmings for both of them. Being Texas, the portions were huge.

"Are you hungry?" Bolan asked.

"Let us hope so," Pilar said, then surprised Bolan by attacking the meal with enthusiasm.

"How did it happen between you and Don?"

"We met because of Tomas. He brought Don home one day. They had become quite close." Pilar's cheeks flushed at the memory. "Almost immediately there was a connection. Neither of us expected it, and Don was reluctant to let it happen because of his job. But people sometimes cannot fight these things. I believe Don saw how I hated what Tomas did for Dembrow. After our relationship became more than simple attraction..." She looked Bolan in the eye. "You understand?"

"I understand," he said. "He was a lucky man, Pilar. I'm sorry it ended the way it did."

"Don was a very honest person. He told me why he was here and what he was trying to do. He wanted to end our relationship because of Tomas, but I told him how I felt about Dembrow and his operation. That I wanted Tomas to break away. He said he would do what he could, but made no promises."

"It must have been difficult for you both."

"Yes. But by then it was too late for Don to simply walk away. He was too deeply involved. Both of us knew that if Dembrow found out he would order us both killed. Don told me he had a final piece of information to collect, then he would call in his people. He had to be careful with what he had found. It was becoming harder for him to pass on his findings to his people. Don suspected there was someone in the local department on Dembrow's payroll. We had planned to move away after his assignment was over, but I believe Tomas found out about us at the same time he learned who Don really was. Two days after that Don vanished without a word. Tomas came to me and told me what he had done. He said that because we were family he had told Dembrow's people to leave me alone. But he would be watching in case I did anything foolish. I did not know what I should do." She shook her head in despair. "My own brother. He has become so involved with the Rojas Cartel that nothing is sacred to him any longer. He has become poisoned by their evil. Now I would not be surprised by anything he does."

3

"We spotted them," Dante said into his cell phone. "The guy with her fits the description we got from Lucas when we spoke to him at the hospital. He's the one who attacked him and Diaz. They're going into the diner on Avalon. They came out of the motel up the street."

"Okay. Wait for backup, then deal with them. That son of a bitch could be DEA, picking up where that other bastard left off. We'll be with you in a couple of minutes. Send one guy around back to deal with the diner staff, then go in the front door and waste them both. I don't want this fucking mess to get any bigger than it already is. Boss man is pissed enough because of that undercover agent. Right now we've got to close this down."

"Another hit so soon? You don't figure this will piss him off even more?"

"More than that fuckin' Mex spilling her guts to a Fed? Wake up, Dante. This needs the door slammin' on it before it ends up on the news."

"I guess."

"Don't guess. I'll drop the guys up the block from where you are. Pick them up and hit that diner now. I'll tell Dembrow to make sure we're all covered."

"I'm not so sure I like that," Dante said.

"What?"

"The thought where you figure we need covering."

"Dante, just do it, or it'll be your sorry ass in a sling."

"JESUS," DEMBROW YELLED. "I don't want you going round shooting up the whole goddamn town. When I said find the girl and the guy with her, I meant bring them in alive so we can talk to them."

"Mr. Dembrow, I figured the best was if they were dead. Then we're rid of the problem."

"Peck, you don't make decisions without passing it by me." Dembrow slammed his hand down on his desk. "Call Dante. Pull the fuckin' crew out before this happens. Do it now."

Dante tapped the cell phone's keypad. He heard the other phone ring, and keep ringing—and he knew he was too late.

4

Pilar paused, pushing away the remains of her meal. Bolan asked the waitress for more coffee. He felt for the young woman. Her life had been dramatically changed following the death of Manners, and the soldier understood her situation. The man she had loved had been snatched from her, and her own brother had the responsibility for that. He would not have liked to have been in that position.

"Since Tomas has gone across the border to see Rojas, I finally went back to Don's apartment. It was torn apart. Dembrow's people had been there. Perhaps they believed Don had left information lying around. They are that stupid. Did they expect he would display his reports for them to find?" She sat upright, thrusting her hands through her dark hair, shaking her head. "I could have cried when I saw what they had done to his apartment. It wasn't much, but we had spent good times there. Then I found the lighter on the floor where it had been scattered with other things. I took a few personal items and wrapped them in a bundle. It was only as I walked away that those two followed me."

"And that was when I showed up."

"Lucky for me." She smiled, raising her coffee cup. "I want to know how I can help. What can I tell you about Dembrow's organization? Or Rojas?"

"All you know. Or believe you know."

A sixth sense made Bolan's combat senses flair. Something had altered the mood of the diner, and when he glanced beyond Pilar he saw that the diner was deserted. The waitress and the cook from the kitchen had vanished.

Bolan reached behind him and eased out the P-226. As he brought his hand to the front, Pilar's eyes widened at the sight of the weapon.

A moving shadow caught Bolan's eye. Someone moved into view from the kitchen. The guy cleared the edge of the serving shelf. He carried a shotgun, the muzzle rising.

Bolan's reaction was pure and simple. He two-fisted the SIG and triggered three fast shots. The 9 mm slugs centered in the guy's chest, knocking him back. His hands jerked the shotgun up and it fired at the diner's ceiling. Shots blasted at one of the light fittings, sparks showering as the fluorescent tubes exploded.

The door to the diner burst open, a lean figure stepping inside. The guy carried an SMG and he opened fire as the muzzle tracked in.

Bolan had reached out to grab Pilar and haul her out of the line of fire, but his action was a second too late. In a frozen moment of clarity he saw the coffee cup in her hand explode, the dark liquid shearing into fine drops. The line of slugs traveled along her arm and across her chest, the brutal impact shredding cloth and puncturing flesh. Gouts of blood flew everywhere as she was twisted under the impact. The stunned expression on Pilar's beautiful face was suddenly obscured as the spray of slugs ripped into her jaw and cheek, taking away bone and tissue. Then her thick mass of black hair swung wildly in the instant before the top of her head exploded, blood and brain matter misting the air.

5

Rage at the wanton destruction of a young life fueled Bolan's actions. Even as Pilar's slender body fell back, the Executioner dropped to one knee below the level of the table. He took a single, hard breath, then launched himself from cover, knowing his move had gained him scant seconds. The gunner would be angling away from the door, seeking to regain his target. Bolan wasn't about to allow him any leeway.

He heard the thump of booted feet on the diner floor and saw the guy's lower legs in the gap between booths. Bolan snapped the SIG around, extended his right arm and put single shots into the guy's knees, the 9 mm slugs shattering bone and dropping the shooter to the floor. As he stumbled, yelling in pain, the hardman came face-to-face with his attacker, and the intense look in the Executioner's eyes told the man his life was at an end. He threw out one hand as if to plead for mercy, but his supplication was ignored. Bolan hit him with a triple volley that caved in his face and cored into his brain.

Bolan powered up off the floor, tucking the SIG back behind his belt and snatching up the abandoned SMG, an H&K MP-5. He noted the taped second magazine as he straightened and, checking the diner's frontage, saw the black SUV parked at an angle on the diner's lot, its doors gaping open. Three more armed figures were closing on the eatery, weapons up, confirming they were not stopping in for coffee.

As the lead gunner mounted the steps, Bolan triggered the SMG through the glass of the door. Glittering shards blew out, mingling with the sustained burst of automatic fire. The guy took the full force in his midsection, the volley tearing at his insides. A few 9 mm rounds blew out at the base of his spine, the impact of the burst wrenching him off the steps and depositing his writhing form on the pavement.

Bolan kicked the door, bursting into the open, and immediately engaged the other shooters. His MP-5 stuttered in a harsh rattle, his shots catching the pair before they could react in any substantial way. Bolan put them down with cold efficiency. He coolly changed magazines as the first clicked empty, then raked the bloody pair on the pavement again before turning the SMG on the SUV. The soldier hit the vehicle with the rest of the magazine, shredding tires, shattering windows and puncturing the gleaming bodywork.

When all the gunners had been silenced, he stood for a moment, the SMG's muzzle pointed at the ground, then he turned and went back inside the diner. He paused briefly beside Pilar's still form, checking her pulse and finding none, as he had expected.

"I let you down, Pilar Trujillo. Forgive me for that. But I'll see this through, and that's a promise."

He walked behind the counter, through the kitchen and out the rear door. Bolan kept to the shadows, working his way back to the motel, breaking down the SMG as he went, throwing parts in all directions until he had discarded the weapon. His prints weren't on file—thanks to the cybercrew at the Farm, so he wasn't worried about that. He picked up the distant wail of sirens, so he stayed on the back lots, finally slipping inside the motel grounds and easing through the shadows to reach the path that led to the rooms. By the time he let himself back into his room, his anger had subsided to a controllable level.

But the sensation of loss hadn't.

Pilar's death would be with him for a while. Once again

an innocent had died because she had become involved in the soulless determination of Evil to protect itself against exposure. Siding with Manners had drawn the young woman into the line of fire. Her enemies had tracked her, taking her life as casually as flicking off a light switch. Only this time they had not taken into account the response of the man with her. Bolan had already been involved in the matter, but his resolve had been strengthened by her death, a needless, unnecessary, cruel death. A vibrant young woman had been destroyed through greed and the hunger for power.

For Bolan, her death would offer yet another ghost to join the others. Though he had long ago accepted the dreams that sometimes visited him in the long dark nights, each new visitation simply affirmed the commitment he had made when he embarked on his War Everlasting.

The Executioner seldom dreamed about the enemies he had killed. Usually it was those who had been caught up in the violence through no fault of their own. He called them his friendly ghosts.

Bolan checked the motel courtyard through the window shutters. People were emerging from rooms, moving toward the street. He dropped the pistol into his carry-all, then he unbuttoned his shirt and ruffled his hair, opened his door and stepped outside, merging with the curious motel guests.

"What's going on?" he asked, feigning a sleepy voice.

The young couple he had spoken to shrugged.

"Sounded like shooting," the man said.

Bolan drifted along with the curious until they were stopped by uniformed police officers.

Standing in the crowd, Bolan cast a keen eye on the scene outside the diner. A number of police cruisers were parked on the street, their lights flashing. More sirens could be heard approaching the area. An ambulance, then a second, rolled in. A couple of minutes later a local TV station mobile unit showed up, and the event turned into a public spectacle. Bolan made sure he remained in the background in case any probing camera was turned in his direction.

Someone demanded to know what was going on.

"All we know, ma'am, is there's been some shooting," the lanky cop drawled. "Can't tell you more 'cause we don't know anything else."

A couple of unmarked police cars showed up, plainclothes detectives moving in to take charge. More uniforms arrived, reinforcements to help hold back the crowd that was increasing. Bolan saw the crime scene investigation van roll up. Nothing would happen now until the CSI team had tagged and bagged the scene, outside and inside the diner.

The young couple Bolan had seen from the motel appeared at his side. The woman held herself close to the man.

"Did you see those bodies?" she said. "It looked just awful. We only stopped for overnight, and we'll be glad to leave in the morning."

"I heard somebody saying it was most likely something to do with drugs," the man said. "You reckon it could be so?"

"Maybe," Bolan said.

He turned away and walked back in the direction of the motel. As he crossed the courtyard the manager stepped out of his office.

"You see what happened?"

"Looks like some shooting at the diner."

"Oh."

Bolan made his way to his room and let himself back inside. He quickly packed, conscious of how the situation in town had changed. His closeness to Pilar's death might easily compromise his presence. If anyone connected him to her, his anonymity might end. He couldn't afford to come under police scrutiny.

He ran back over his activity since he and Pilar had arrived at the motel. It had already been dark and he had parked in close to the room, letting Pilar slip into the shadows as she left the vehicle. As far as he could recall, no one had been around when they had walked across the courtyard and onto the street. The only individual who might have seen them was the motel manager as they passed his office window. Their short walk to the diner had been along a deserted street due to the lateness of the hour. Bolan remembered the waitress in the diner. She had seen them together, and she might be able to provide the local LEOs with a description. Bolan knew he was going to need to move on, but he was not going to be able to do that so easily. Not with the local law camped just outside along the street.

A sudden thought came to him. Bolan crossed the room and turned on the TV. He used the remote to find the local station and found himself looking at the very scene he had just left. He upped the volume and heard a voice-over describing the scene.

"...have here are multiple killings. Three bodies outside the diner. Inside, the shocking discovery of three more. Two men and a young Latina all shot to death. The diner's owner and waitress were found locked inside the cold room. I managed a few words with Homicide Detective Clarke Whittington, and he told me that at this moment the police cannot say what lies behind this tragedy. It is too early in the investigation to offer a reason..."

Bolan clicked off the TV, took out his cell phone and called Stony Man Farm. Brognola answered, admitting he had been watching the incident unfold on TV.

"Looks like you got trouble down there, Striker. Yeah, we've been monitoring the local TV station seeing that you were in the area. I have to admit they're sometimes faster at reporting events than our sources."

Bolan gave a short review of the night's occurrences.

"I'm not off the hook yet," he added. "Especially if anyone recalls seeing me in Pilar's company. I'm going to have to relocate, but I can't do much about it until morning. The diner's a short walk from my motel, and the place is overrun by the local cops at the moment."

"We'll do what we can to scupper any potential threat," Brognola said. "Aaron's team will monitor all police frequencies, and the genius himself is trying to access the local computer system even as we speak." The big Fed was referring to Aaron "the Bear" Kurtzman, head of the cyberteam at Stony Man Farm.

"Any result from that intel I queried earlier?"

"Yeah," Brognola growled. "And you're going to love this. It's a Moscow telephone number. The Bear couldn't get much joy apart from the location, so he made a call to your OCD pal, Valentine Seminov. It seems the number belongs to someone Seminov has been chasing for some time. A guy called Vash Bondarchik. He's a big-time arms dealer, who's well connected. Russian Mafia. He has clients worldwide. Seminov asked if he could help, and I said I would pass his request on."

"I'll bear that in mind. What about the name on the slip? Calderon?"

"Hermano Calderon. He works for Benito Rojas, handling technical matters. Weapons and such. Our friends at the DEA have a nice fat file on him, and the Bear somehow managed some cyber sleight-of-hand and downloaded it. Could be the guy to work these missiles for Rojas. Calderon is a little careless with his cell phone calls. Bear got into his call list and it appears he's made a few to Bondarchik over the past few weeks. Also to the cell phone used by one Tibor Danko. Danko is Bondarchik's SIC. Seminov knows the guy and says he's a smart piece of work, which was the closest translation he could offer without resorting to really bad language."

"Hell of a mix there," Bolan said. "Something I can work on. Listen, I'll move in the morning and make some distance from here. Monitor the situation and update me."

"Yeah. Striker. Are you going to be okay?"

"I'll be fine."

"Sorry about the young woman."

"Not as sorry as the bastards who put out the hit are going to be," Bolan said.

6

Marshal Dembrow was in top form, his powerful voice at full pitch as he berated the members of his local crew. Physically he was an impressive figure, topping the six-foot mark by a good three inches, his broad, less than handsome face darkened with his fury. The rest of his body was in proportion to his height. He was a fitness fanatic, working out every day in the expensively equipped gym attached to his spacious house. He also trained in martial arts, so the concept of being able to break bones was well within his ability. Not that he needed to use physical force—he paid people to do that for him. But he had done the deed himself on occasion.

At the moment, the thunder of his voice had the crew members subdued. They were all tough, but they might as well have been children as they stood ranged in front of Dembrow's desk. They were his men. He paid them well—very well—and provided whatever they needed. All he asked for in return was loyalty and a commitment to the business they were in. He got it. His people were in for the duration. As ruthless as they were in the pursuit of the Rojas Cartel's needs, they were cowed as Dembrow ranted at them for turning a simple expedition into a total disaster.

As his rage subsided and the invective he spewed began to slow, Dembrow felt his control returning. He ran a hand through his collar-length blond hair and fixed his crew with a hard stare, delivering his concluding words.

"This isn't what I pay you sons of bitches for. One guy. One fucking guy and he's making all of you look like a bunch of mouth-breathin' peckerwoods. This guy is smart, and he can handle himself. Just look what he did to Dante's crew at the diner. One man, and he put them all down. Now I'm going to say it one more time. Nothing gets done until I give the say-so. Understand? I give the orders—you carry them out. For the moment walk easy. I don't want the town getting too jumpy. If that happens, the cops will have to start rousting us, and I have enough to worry about. I'll have this mother dealt with *my* way."

The moment Dembrow stopped ranting the subdued group turned and left the study, the last man out closing the door.

Dembrow leaned on his hands, his head hanging. Willing himself to calm down, he took deep breaths, sucking air deep into his lungs and exhaling slowly. His anger finally contained, he stood and crossed to the well-stocked wet bar in the corner of the expansive, richly furnished room. He opened the glass-fronted cooler and took out a chilled bottle of beer, removed the cap and enjoyed a long swallow. The cold liquid didn't satisfy him as it usually did, a sure sign that Dembrow was far from happy. He took out a second bottle and returned to slump behind his desk.

"Son of a bitch," he muttered. He drained the first bottle and opened the second.

The silent figure in the high-backed deep leather recliner facing the room's big window slowly eased it around so he could see Dembrow. He had remained unheard and unseen during Dembrow's bawling out of his crew. He stood and crossed to the bar, helping himself to a large tumbler of vintage bourbon.

Tall, lean, his thick dark hair framing a hollow-cheeked face, he wore all black and moved with a languorous grace. He sat down again, swirling the bourbon in the tumbler, breathing in the fumes.

His name was Billy Joe Rankin. He was Dembrow's closest

adviser, a thinker who viewed a problem from all angles before he offered any kind of advice.

"You want my opinion, Marshal? Get on the phone and call in Preacher and Choirboy. Turn those homicidal maniacs loose. This is their kind of work."

"Dammit, Billy Joe, I don't need this right now."

"Marshal, this is a bad patch you're going through. It'll pass. Hey, you've gone through times like this before."

"Oh, sure. This time I let a damned Fed into my organization. He skims off information they can maybe use against me and almost walks away with it."

"But he didn't. Manners is dead, and the Feds still don't have any kind of case against you. Let that ride. If anything does rise to the surface, we'll let the lawyers handle it. Believe me, Marshal, this is going away."

"Not until I know who this bastard is."

"That's something we all want to know."

"Is he a damn Fed? A cop? Some psycho on a mission from God?"

"You want to find out?"

"Well, yeah, that seems to be a good idea."

"Then do what I say. Let your boys run around making noises, but sic Preacher and Choirboy on him. Toss them a contract and let them run."

Dembrow reached for one of the phones on his desk, tapped in a number and waited while it rang out. The voice on the other end was immediately recognizable.

"Preacher. You want to take a run over? I got a proposition for you two. Big payday. Huge payday. Well, hell, of course the usual. Half down if you come on board. The rest when you deliver. Sure, I'll be here."

Rankin poured himself another drink. He stood at the big window overlooking the grounds of Dembrow's large property.

"It's time you put that swimming pool in, Marshal. It'll make a nice addition to the place. We can cut a good deal with Jack Templeton."

"You think?"

"Big pool. Patio surround. Spot for a barbecue. Damn good way to entertain business clients. Have a few pretty girls running around in bikinis. Or no bikinis."

Dembrow laughed. "Hey, you could be right, Billy Joe. What the hell, like you said, we got the cash. Give Templeton a call. Set it up."

Rankin sipped his bourbon, his mission accomplished. Dembrow's mind had been diverted from his current problems. His employer was a hard man when it came to his business dealings, but he had a failing that caused him to worry overly when problems came his way. If Dembrow allowed himself to be drawn away from his main concerns, the drug business might suffer, and no one in the organization wanted that. Especially Rankin. He enjoyed the success of Dembrow's dealings and the material gains that he enjoyed. He wanted it to stay that way, so it was part of his job to keep Dembrow on a linear path, fielding off anything that might rock the boat.

PREACHER AND CHOIRBOY showed up an hour later. They parked a gleaming 1986 Lincoln Continental in the drive and stepped out, clad in tailored Western-style suits, complete with leather boots and wide brimmed Stetson hats. They were every inch Texan boys, down to the expensive aviator shades and string ties. The Mexican houseman let them in and escorted them through the house. Dembrow was in his office, alone, Rankin attending to other business. The pair settled into the big armchairs ranged in front of Dembrow's desk. The houseman took their hats. Dembrow handed them ice-cold bottles of beer, then settled back in his own chair.

"Nice job you boys did on that Fed. I think we got the message across."

"Take a man's money, it's only right you give him value," Preacher said.

Reaching down behind his desk Dembrow lifted a tan leather carry-all. He placed it on the desk and slid it in Preacher's direction.

"Well, guys, it's time for you to do it again."

Preacher took the bag and placed it on the floor between the armchairs.

"You heard about the shooting at the diner?" Dembrow asked.

Choirboy nodded. "Kind of ended up messy."

"That was a local fuckup," Dembrow said. "Some of the hired help decided to think for themselves and take out the girl the undercover Fed had been bedding. Figured they were doing me a big favor. All they did was screw up and make the situation worse."

"The way we heard it, the girl had some protection," Preacher said.

"Damn right. He spread my crew all over the scene and walked away. "

"He our target?"

"I've run some checks, and no one seems to know who this bastard is."

"Nothing from the local law-enforcement agencies?"

"I had a word with my contacts at local and State. Not a whisper. If this guy is undercover, he's so deep he's invisible."

Preacher drained his beer. "If the Feds have put in another agent so soon after the last one, he won't be making himself known. And he isn't about to make any new friends. That means he's working in the cold. He'll be a stranger. That could work for us. Folks around these parts don't buddy up so fast. They tend to be suspicious if you're not a native." He pushed to his feet. "You leave it to us, Mr. Dembrow. We'll find your boy and retire him."

Choirboy picked up the money bag.

"I'll keep you posted," he said.

7

Choirboy placed the leather bag in the Lincoln's trunk. When he climbed into the car, Preacher had the vehicle running, the powerful engine softly purring. Choirboy sank back in the soft seat, tipping his hat forward over his face.

"When you reckon you have the strength," Preacher said, "give me some thoughts."

"If we're goin' to find this boy, we need a starting point. How about the diner? He was there. He took out Dembrow's crew. Somebody had to have seen him."

"Good thinking, son. It's the diner, then."

They waited until dark. At 11:15 p.m., the parking lot was empty. The staff parked up at the rear of the establishment. Preacher coasted onto the lot, the Lincoln's lights already turned off. Choirboy followed him out of the car and they walked down the side of the building, looking for the back entrance. The kitchen door was ajar against the night heat. There were two cars parked in back.

"Let's do it, son," Preacher said, leading the way in.

The diner's kitchen hung on to the day's cooking smells. A wall air conditioner pushed out barely chilled air, rattling as it worked. The owner, middle-aged and thickset, hunched over a deep fat fryer as he cleaned it. The back of his T-shirt clung to his skin, patches of sweat darkening the cotton.

"They say industrial kitchens can be dangerous places," Preacher said conversationally as he moved up behind the man.

The man straightened and looked at Preacher and Choirboy. There was no mistaking the implicit threat in Preacher's voice, so the man simply stood there.

Choirboy walked directly past, skirting the edge of the kitchen and emerging in the dining area to confront the waitress, who was clearing tables. She froze when she saw Choirboy, her eyes suddenly wide, swiveling toward the diner's entrance. The damaged door had already been replaced since the shooting.

As Choirboy shook his head at her, he crossed to the door and locked it, then stood with his back to it as Preacher and the owner appeared.

"Both of you sit down," Preacher said. "This ain't gonna take long."

"If this is about the shooting, we already told the cops everything we know," the owner said.

"Let's make this quick, then. You were both here that night?"

"Yes," the woman said. She was in her early forties, not unattractive, but starting to show her age. She kept brushing loose strands of hair back from her cheek.

"The man and woman who came in—did you know them?"

"No, sir. Both were strangers to me," she said, and the owner nodded his agreement.

"Tell me about the man."

"Tall. Black hair and blue eyes. Handsome looking guy in a rugged sort of way. And he looked like he would be able to handle himself. Polite, too."

"See, that wasn't hard," Preacher said. "And you gave a good description, ma'am."

"Something that comes with the job," she said. "You get to check people over. Try to spot potential problem customers. I guess it's a habit."

"Did they drive onto the lot?"

"No. I only noticed that after they'd already ordered, because two of our regulars left and drove away and the lot was empty. I didn't have time to think about it, what with everything that happened."

"So the guy and the girl must have walked here?"

"I guess so."

"Unusual," Preacher said. "Folk don't make a habit of walking the streets around here."

"So where did they come from?" Choirboy asked.

"Likely the motel," the owner suggested.

"Motel?"

"Out of the parking lot, make a left and it's a couple hundred yards on the same side of the street."

The waitress nodded in agreement. "That's right. We get folks staying there coming in to eat. Hardly worth driving, it being so close."

"You tell the cops that?"

"Ed and me told them nothing. The way they treated us, the hell with them," the woman said.

Preacher glanced at his partner. Choirboy smiled.

"How did the shooting go down?" Preacher asked out of professional curiosity.

"We didn't see it," the woman said. "An armed man came in through the kitchen door. He pushed Ed and me into the big cold room and locked the door. Said if we raised any fuss he'd shoot us."

"Next thing we heard," Ed said, "was like a war had broken out. Lots of gunfire."

"After that it just went real quiet. We didn't know what was going on, so we stayed quiet, too."

"When the cops came and started shouting, we hollered and they let us out. Bastards treated us like we were part of it," Ed grumbled, obviously still resenting the treatment he'd received at the hands of the local police. "Questioned us half the damn night, and us still shivering from that cold room."

"Is that all you wanted?" the waitress asked.

Preacher could see she was trembling.

"That's all, ma'am. Hope we haven't upset you too much.

We're going now." He turned away, then paused to look back. "That thing you mentioned?"

"What?"

"Being able to remember details about customers and all?"

The waitress managed a thin smile. "It doesn't seem to be working tonight," she said, understanding the reasoning behind Preacher's question. "Could be because I'm at the end of my shift."

Preacher raised his hands. "Lucky for us then."

BACK IN THE CAR Choirboy said, "Nice folks."

"Yep."

Preacher turned onto the street and coasted along until he saw the lights of the motel. He made a left and rolled the Lincoln across the courtyard, coming to stop outside the manager's office. Through the window he could see the guy on duty watching TV.

"Come in the back way," he said. "I'll go talk to the guy."

The motel manager didn't even look up from his TV as Preacher entered the airless office. He simply waved a hand.

"You want a room?"

"Just some information."

Now the man glanced up, irritation on his face.

"Do I look like a fucking tourist guide?"

Preacher smiled. "Remember I asked politely."

"I'll put you down for an award. If you don't want a room, I'm busy."

"This could have gone a lot easier, son," Preacher said.

"Just get the hell out of here 'fore I—"

"Before you what, boy?" Choirboy asked.

He had walked around to the rear of the office, coming in through the screen door and had moved up beside the manager. He pressed the muzzle of his handgun against the guy's skull.

"I asked nicely," Preacher said, "but this cocky son of a bitch decided to get lippy."

He turned and locked the door, closing the blind.

"You know what?" Choirboy said. "I recognize this bird.

He used to work for Harry Lyle out of Dallas. You recall that place Lyle had downtown? This guy used to work behind the bar, but Harry caught him shortchanging customers. Had him worked over and run out of town. They called him Hatcher. Nick Hatcher."

"I do believe you're right there, son." Preacher leaned against the desk. "He was a lippy bastard then. No grace in him at all."

"Yeah, well, I don't work for Lyle anymore," Hatcher said. "But I do work for someone a damn sight harder, so you better lay off me."

Preacher's eyes raised to Choirboy's face and smiled. No words were needed. Choirboy used his pistol to remind Hatcher he was in no position to make threats. The meaty slam of the steel against Hatcher's head delivered the message. Hatcher grunted, sliding from his seat after the third blow and landed on his knees, his head hanging. Blood ran down his neck and soaked the collar of his shirt. More dripped to the floor. Preacher joined Choirboy behind the desk, and together they hauled the dazed Hatcher back into his seat. Hatcher stared up into Preacher's face, still defiant. The killer sighed, then without warning he punched Hatcher in the face a few times, rocking the man's head back. Blood spattered Hatcher's features, and he would have slid out of the chair again if Choirboy hadn't caught hold of his shoulders and pulled him back.

"Don't make the mistake of believing I give a rat's ass who you work for," Preacher said after a while. "Anything that even smells of a threat kind of gets me all upset, son."

"Take heed of that," Choirboy said from behind Hatcher. "He gets kind of unstable if someone threatens him." He slapped Hatcher on the shoulder. "You should have been nice to the man. We would have been long gone by now, and you could be back watching your movie."

"So what is it you want?" Hatcher asked. His words were muffled due to the bloody state of his lips and a couple of loose teeth. Blood dribbled from his mouth as he spoke.

"Night of the diner shooting. You had a guest here. Big guy.

Tall. Black hair. Blue eyes. He could have walked to the diner. Had a girl with him. Pretty. Mexican. She was the one who got shot and killed. You recall?"

Hatcher considered the question, sucking air noisily into his battered mouth. He seemed to be having trouble focusing on Preacher's face, but he eventually nodded.

"Only stayed a couple of nights. Left the day after the shooting. I never seen him with no girl. I don't notice everyone who walks by."

"Now that wasn't hard, was it?" Choirboy asked.

Hatcher pushed to his feet, wobbling unsteadily, and made his way to the file box on the desk. He rifled through the cards until he found the one he wanted, passed it to Preacher, then sank back into his seat. Preacher slid the card into his pocket after a quick look.

"His vehicle? What was the make and model?"

"Late model Ford 4x4. Dark red. License number's on the card. The guy calls himself Matt Cooper."

"Been a pleasure doing business with you, Nick," Preacher said. "We'll go now. Leave you to your business. Here's a word of advice. Don't even consider bringing the cops in. It wouldn't do you any good. Tell your boss what happened if you feel you need to." Preacher smoothed down his jacket. "If you do, tell him Preacher said hello. He'll understand."

Hatcher watched them leave, his eyes already glazing over, sliding back down in his seat.

Choirboy led the way out through the back door. They walked around to the waiting Lincoln. Choirboy got behind the wheel and Preacher settled beside him.

"Which way?" Choirboy asked.

"You choose, son. I got a few calls to make." Preacher took out the registration card and held it up. "We got some tracking to do, but first I need to get us a little direction."

While Choirboy cruised, Preacher tapped in a number and held his cell phone to his ear.

"Clarence, I need you to check out a license-plate number for me." He read out the details. "Soon as, son. This is urgent. Call me." Preacher redialed and asked to speak to Dembrow. "His name is Matt Cooper. That's all we got up to now, but it'll do."

He ended the call.

"If this yahoo ain't an undercover cop," Choirboy said, "who the hell is he?"

Preacher considered. "Good question, son. I'll ask when we find him."

"Maybe he's some covert military specialist. Delta Force. SEAL. Sent in by the government so he don't have to be answerable to anyone."

"Son, you amaze me sometimes," Preacher said. "It could be you've lit on the right number. DEA and the like don't have those kind of skills. They ain't trained in such business. But the military teach their special forces just the way our boy acts."

"Likely then he won't be easy to find."

"Oh, hell, son, it wouldn't be fun if it was easy."

8

"Local cops have put the shooting down as gang related," Brognola explained. "It wouldn't be the first time drug factions have fallen out and tried to clean house."

"So they won't be digging too deep?" Bolan asked.

"They'll go through the motions. Open a file and log in all the details. Truth be told, Striker, a few dead traffickers aren't going to merit a big-time operation. On past experience the police know they'll get no help from anyone. Local criminals will pull in their heads and stay quiet. Questions will get the cops *nada*. Somewhere along the line the file will end up in the cold case drawer."

"What about Pilar?"

"They know she was related to Tomas Trujillo, so she's being treated as a hostile. A member of the Rojas Cartel. And before you say it sucks, Striker, let's go with it for now."

"How do I fit in? Any story on my presence?"

"They have you down as a cartel goon, there to look after the girl."

"Whoever I'm supposed to be I don't come over as good at my job," Bolan said. "Pilar is dead either way."

"Quit that, Striker. You did what you could at the time. No blame."

"I blame myself. You know how I feel about innocents getting caught up in these things."

"I know, and I wish I could make it right for you."

"These bastards spread their violence around like confetti at a wedding, Hal, and they don't give a damn who gets dragged into the line of fire."

"Which is why we're doing what we can to put them down."

"What about Don Manners? Is the DEA going to put his death in a cold case file?"

"They won't quit. But what have they got to go on? No witnesses. Manners was undercover, so all the feedback they have is his own. Dammit, Striker, it's why you're there." Brognola's last words were delivered with a hard edge, almost hinting that Bolan was the one with all the answers.

The Executioner let his friend's frustration wash over him. He understood the big Fed's mood. Like Bolan, Hal Brognola accepted every loss personally. He worked the edge all the time, aware of the way the game was played—hard investigations that often produced minimal results and were frequently closed due to the death of courageous men and women. Brognola was a man of courage himself, and he carried the burden on his broad shoulders.

The brief silence was broken when Brognola cleared his throat, his voice gruff as he said, "You didn't deserve that, Striker."

"I'll try not to lose any sleep over it," Bolan said lightly. "Did Manners point the finger at any local cops who might be on the Rojas payroll?"

"I've been going over the file reports the President delivered. Manners did talk about one in particular. A Deputy Chris Malloy. He works out of the narcotics squad for the county sheriff's department, which is headquartered in a town called Cooter's Crossing."

"Having a man right on the inside could come in handy for the cartel."

"Damn right it could. I had the cyberteam run a profile on the guy. They dug into Malloy's personal computer files and uncovered a hidden folder. Malloy is computer smart, but there was no way he could stop Akira from breaking his encryptions. Malloy has a couple of bank accounts under a false name, and he gets regular deposits. Generous amounts, too. Akira followed the trail and traced the deposits back to a guy named Eugene Corey." Akira Tokaido was the Farm's top computer hacker.

"And?"

"Corey's main business is a very successful vehicle franchise in the area. Anything from autos to trucks to big rigs. He has sites all around the country. He buys, sells, rents and runs ads on TV. 'If it's on wheels—we do the deals.' That's his slogan. Rumor has it, from the DEA files, that Corey supplies transport to the Rojas Cartel as a subsidiary to his main business, and pulls in some big bucks. There's no direct connection, but with the number of sites he has scattered around the county, it's hard to keep track of all vehicle movements. From what Akira's probing has brought to light, it looks like he's also slipped in payola for the cartel as an extra."

"It's somewhere for me to start," Bolan said.

"I'll have the data downloaded to your phone," Brognola said.

"Thanks for that."

"Anything else you need?"

"Work up a file on Bondarchik. If Manners was correct on this weapons shipment to Rojas, it might be helpful if I know how it's being done."

"You'll have it all shortly."

BOLAN CRUISED the highway until he spotted a gas station. He turned in and filled the Ford's big tank. While he was there, he checked water and tire pressure. Inside the convenience store he bought some bottles of water and a handful of health bars. He stored those in the cab, spun the wheel and drove across to the handy diner on the far side of the lot. Falling back on his military training, Bolan decided it was time to have a meal while he waited for Stony Man to send him the data he needed. Eat when you can. Sleep when you can. The enemy wasn't going to give you space if those needs came up at a bad time.

Stepping inside brought back the memory of Pilar Trujillo. Sitting in one of the empty booths, waiting for his food and coffee, Bolan ran through that scenario once again: the chatter as she ate; her brief repose shattered by the bullets that had hammered into her, reducing her from a vibrant young woman to a shattered and disfigured corpse on the floor of the diner.

"You okay?"

Bolan glanced up at the concerned face of the waitress. She slid his plate in front of him and stood with a mug of steaming coffee in her hand.

"I'm fine," he said. "Just working on a problem I have to solve."

She put the mug on the table. "Don't let it kill you, honey."

"That's what I'm working on."

Bolan ate his meal. He was on his second mug of coffee when his phone rang. It was Price this time.

"Data download will follow from this call," she said. "There's a small town twenty miles from your location. Your guy Corey has a big franchise there, because the town is a hub for rail freight distribution. It's a kind of a crossroads in the area. Freight is shipped in and out by road and rail, which means it's a busy junction. Manners mentioned it in his final report. He had the feeling it was one of the jumping-off points for the cartel."

"Cooter's Crossing?"

"You know I hate it when you do that. How did you know?"

"Hal mentioned it when we last spoke. But all he gave me was the name of the place."

"A guy named Abe Cooter first set up the place back in the late 1800s. With all the cattle business and the railhead, he figured there was money to be made. And he was right. He lived until he was in his nineties and died a millionaire. There are still some cattle ranches around the area now. Cooter's Crossing has a reputation as a tough town, so watch your back, Striker. That Deputy Malloy is down as a tough guy."

"I'll watch out for him. Remind me how you knew where I

was?" Bolan asked, curiosity spiking, tinged with a little unease because he had a feeling he already knew the answer.

"Your rental," Price said, "has a LoJack system built in. It's standard in most new vehicles these days. Why?"

"Because if you can track me, so can the opposition if they get my license number."

"How would they know that?"

"These people know how to find things out. They have their methods."

"Damn, Striker, they could have a tail on you already. Is it time to lose your truck?"

"Not yet. Maybe it's time to let them show themselves."

"Is that a good idea?"

"We'll see," Bolan said. "Download my stuff and stop frowning."

"I'm not frown… Hey, how did you know?"

Bolan chuckled gently. "You just told me."

Price said her goodbyes and hit the button that sent the data to Bolan's cell phone. He read it while he drank his third mug of coffee. By the time he left the diner and returned to his truck, he had enough on Eugene Corey to warrant a close inspection of the man and his business.

9

Cooter's Crossing turned out to be larger than Bolan had expected. It had a modest financial district that housed banks and legal operations. He cruised through the center, following the main street until he spotted a modern hotel in the retail district. The soldier drove into the parking lot, took his luggage and walked inside. He was greeted by the smiling receptionist who quickly assured him they could find him a room. Minutes later the Executioner was in the elevator and on his way to the fourth floor, with the smiling bellman carrying Bolan's clothing bag, while Bolan hung on to the one that held his ordnance.

"First time in the Crossing?" the bellman asked. There was no mistaking his local accent.

"First time," Bolan said.

"Business, or pleasure?"

Bolan thought about that. "You could say business," he said.

"Busy town. You'll find plenty going on."

Bolan nodded. That would be a fact if he had anything to do with it.

The bellman, who had introduced himself as Sam by this time, led Bolan along the thickly carpeted corridor. He stopped at a room and used the key card to open the door. Bolan followed him inside, placed his bag to one side and allowed Sam to complete his task of explaining the amenities.

"Anything I can do, just call, sir."

Bolan handed him a ten-dollar tip and assured Sam he would, then said, "How about a pot of fresh coffee? Can't get on with that complimentary stuff."

The banknote vanished into Sam's pocket. "I'll handle that for you, sir."

Once he was alone, Bolan opened his weapons carry-all and took out his cell phone and made a call to Stony Man Farm. When Price answered he updated her on his status.

"Nice hotel?" she asked.

"You'll find out when my credit-card statement shows up." Which was a standard joke between them. Bolan's credit cards were preloaded so that there was no paper trail.

Price made a disapproving sound. "On company expenses, too?"

"It's lonely on the road."

"Mmm. I'm sending you a contact number for Seminov."

"Thanks. You got anything else for me?"

"This may be something or nothing. The cyberteam was trawling all local police sources and they came across this. A guest at the motel you used called the police when they found the manager injured. The manager refused to make any kind of statement. He said he'd had a fall, but passed out on them. Cops took him to a local emergency room. The guy was treated but still insisted on no statement. He refused to give them any information, so they had to let him go. Bear followed through and checked the attending officer's computer report. The cop said it looked like the man had been pistol whipped around the head and hit in the face. There was nothing else they could do, so the file was logged and that was it. The guy's name is Nick Hatcher. He has a file. Nothing serious. He's just a petty criminal." Price paused. "What do you think, Striker? Worth anything?"

"Could be someone checking me out, or it could be an unrelated matter."

"Same motel? Close to the diner? I don't like coincidences, Striker. Let's face it, you've caused problems since you showed up in town. And these people are known for being touchy if anything threatens their setup."

"Hatcher at the motel. I'm guessing we know now why he took a beating," Bolan said. "Most likely if they asked about me they would pick up my vehicle details from the registration card. If somebody had a connection in the police department and they ran a make on my truck, that would answer the question. An organization like Dembrow's wouldn't have a problem getting its hands on tracking technology."

"So, who can you trust?" Price asked. "The way I see it, nobody. That makes it hard for you to get information."

"That's what I have you guys for," Bolan said.

"The trouble is, from here we can only yell 'look out.' We can't do a damn thing more."

"Knowing you're there is enough."

"Gee, Striker, you say the sweetest things."

BOLAN WAS STILL recalling the conversation when a tap on his door announced the arrival of his coffee. He sat at the room's desk and ran through all the downloaded data Stony Man Farm had sent him. The accompanying photos Manners had gathered identified Corey and Malloy among a number of the Rojas Cartel's known associates. The person Bolan took initial interest in was one Walter Quinn. The man's rap sheet made interesting reading.

Quinn had been into crime since his teenage years. In and out of prison, association with similar personalities, Quinn had recidivist qualities that made it clear he was never going to clean up his act. He also had a strong proclivity toward violence. During the past few years, he had been involved with Dembrow, and according to Manners, the man was involved in the transportation of drug shipments across the border. Specifically drugs coming from Rojas destined for Dembrow's distribution network. Suspicions, though, were of no use when it came to scoring convictions. Quinn obviously had protection somewhere within the local law. Malloy, perhaps? His back was being covered, and there was also the added fail-safe of legal protection. Any hint of a charge being made brought the instant legal interference that assured Quinn would walk free and clear—which had happened a few times already.

The Executioner's cell phone rang. It was Aaron Kurtzman, the head of Stony Man Farm's technology team, and Bolan went straight to the matter at hand.

"You need something to get you a lever into Dembrow's business?" Kurtzman asked, obviously relishing the moment.

"What have you got?"

"Eugene Corey," Kurtzman said. "Since we scoped him out, I did some more checking, and got a line on his cell phone. I put a trace on his calls, sent and received, and downloaded all his recent calls. He touches base with a guy called Billy Joe Rankin quite a lot. Akira ran a check on Rankin, and the guy is one of Dembrow's buddies. Worked with him for a while. The conversations with Corey are, shall we say, guarded. But guess who they were talking about yesterday?"

"No games, Bear, I'm bushed."

"Okay. Walter Quinn. Bottom line is that Quinn will be getting in touch with Corey. Something about needing wheels for a pickup in a day or two. No specifics but what the hell, Striker, I don't expect Quinn needs transport for a visit to Wal-Mart any time soon."

"Great work, Bear. This could be the break I've been waiting for. Stay on Corey and see if anything else shows up."

"I'll stay tuned."

Bolan helped himself to another coffee as he went over what Kurtzman had just told him. It could turn out to be a real break.

"Time's running out for you, Quinn," Bolan said quietly. "No get out of jail free card this time."

He used his cell phone to call a number that would connect him to someone he knew could provide him with a piece of electronic equipment able to help in the upcoming phase of his mission.

During his long campaigns, with and without official sanction, Bolan had, through necessity, built a small network of covert suppliers of specialist equipment he could call on in times of need. It was not always possible, due to time, distance, and situation, for the Executioner to obtain weapons of war through his normal channels. So Bolan maintained his contacts, and from time-to-time he would call on them. Some were ex-military. A small number were men, even a few women, Bolan had extracted from bad situations, either of their own making, or as a result of what Bolan called misdirection. In the end, they had taken the hand he offered and moved on. The rescued rarely forgot the chance they had been given to step back into the sunlight, and none of his contacts had ever balked at assisting when the call came.

Noah Decard was one of the saved. In the military he had been an electronic warfare specialist. Since his honorable discharge, he had set himself up in the surveillance business, bringing his skills to the commercial market. An unexpected involvement with an organization that was less than honest drew Decard into the murky clutches of violent men. Even though he stood up against the criminal element, Decard came close to losing everything—including his life—until an individual, with a penchant for dispatching lowlifes, came blistering in on a mission takedown. Decard had watched openmouthed as the Executioner had delivered his brand of justice and had brought down their headquarters. In the bloody aftermath, Decard, no fool when it came to recognizing a life-changing moment, had not simply thanked Bolan, but offered the mysterious man in black any help he might need in the future.

Their paths hadn't crossed for a couple of years since Bolan had last made contact, looking for a piece of specialist equipment. The telephone call that came one afternoon caught Decard in his office in San Antonio. The voice he hadn't heard in a while was instantly recognizable.

"Noah."

"Hey. How you doing? I figure this isn't a social call."

"You guessed right."

Decard smiled. "Straight to the heart," he said, smiling. "So what can I do for you?"

Bolan explained in simple words what he needed.

"No problem. Only questions are when and where?"

"ASAP. Couriered to my hotel in Cooter's Crossing." Bolan relayed the address and his cover name.

"I can have it delivered by midmorning tomorrow."

"You can bill me at the same address and I'll settle up later."

"Hey, you trying to spoil our friendship? Who said anything about a bill? Just put it down as my contribution to whatever you're involved in."

"Thanks, Noah. I'm grateful for that."

"You need anything else?"

"That's all this time around."

"You watch yourself down there. I've heard that Cooter's Crossing can be a bad place. Cover your back."

"Will do. And thanks again."

"Anytime, buddy."

THE HOTEL DESK CALLED Bolan's room just after eleven the next morning. A courier had just delivered a package for him. Bolan went down and collected the heavy, shoe-box-sized item. Back in his room he opened the package and took out the contents: a new electronic tracking unit and a number of disc-shaped, magnetic bugs. One of the bugs attached to a vehicle would allow Bolan to follow wherever it traveled without being seen. He would be able to stay well behind the targeted vehicle and see its progress on the tracking unit's GPS monitor.

10

Bolan was able to observe the car dealership without being seen. Across the road from Eugene Corey's business was a shopping mall, and on the second floor a food court where Bolan sat at a terrace café overlooking the road and observed the dealership. Glass-walled walkways ran the length of the mall, and Bolan spent a few hours checking out the comings and goings of Corey's customers and staff. He knew he was taking a chance that might never pay off, but right now it was the only direct lead he had to Quinn and a drug drop, so he decided to allow himself a couple of days staking out the business.

It wasn't the first time Bolan had devoted long hours to staking out the opposition. At least this time he wasn't stretched out in wet grass, or concealed in some dank ditch, waiting for his enemy to show. He was also aware that if he spent too much time inside the mall he might be spotted. Malls were equipped with security cameras. If he was observed spending too much time in the mall, his motives might come under scrutiny. The last thing the Executioner wanted was to be seen and possibly questioned. He'd have to get the Farm to take care of the cameras.

He spent the first day in and around the mall. The second day, dressed in a different set of clothes—bought from the mall—he spent only a couple of hours inside the building, then took his observations outside. The time produced nothing. To his advantage,

Bolan had limitless patience. Late in the morning on the third day, just when it was starting to look as if he would need to come up with a new approach, Walt Quinn showed up.

Bolan was in his Ford, parked in a public parking area just down from Corey's place. The 4x4 was near the perimeter wall of the parking lot. Bolan was about to refresh his parking stub when he saw a metallic blue Toyota sedan turn off the road and cruise past the rows of vehicles for sale. It ignored the customer parking and turned in to a spot at the rear of the main showroom building. Bolan slipped out of his truck and stood near the wall, watching, and recognized Walt Quinn's stocky figure as the man climbed out of the Toyota.

Quinn crossed to the rear of the showroom and went in through a service door. Bolan could see him through the glass-walled structure. The man seemed to know where he was going. He disappeared into an office, emerging minutes later with a tall, sandy-haired man. Bolan knew the face from the downloaded images—Eugene Corey. The pair were talking like old buddies as they returned to the exterior parking area. They crossed to a compound farther in the rear of the main lot, where Corey handed Quinn something. The object turned out to be a set of keys. Quinn raised his hand and pressed a button on the remote. Lights flashed on a light-gray panel truck. The pair spent some more time in conversation before Corey turned and made his way back inside the showroom. Quinn climbed into the truck and reversed it from its spot, then drove off the lot. Bolan started the Ford and exited the parking area. He pulled onto the road four cars down from the panel truck and tailed Quinn.

They drove out of Cooter's Crossing and picked up the main highway leading south. Since the highway was busy, it was easy for Bolan to maintain his tail without being spotted by his quarry.

An hour later they were in open country, with little in the way of an urban landscape to be seen. This was scrub country, dusty and hot. The undulating terrain bordered the highway on each side. Bolan maintained as much distance as he could behind

Quinn, but it was getting harder to maintain multiple vehicles between him and the man.

A truck stop appeared and Quinn angled into the place. Bolan quickly realized this might allow him the opportunity to bug Quinn's truck. He rolled the Ford off the road and parked between two semi-trailers.

He reached for the carry-all and took the GPS tracking bug from the side pocket. He checked the power level. It was at maximum, which would give it at least a twenty-four-hour life. Quinn's panel truck was farther along the line of parked vehicles and as Bolan passed it by he paused briefly, crouched and placed the bug in position at the rear of the panel truck's steel bumper. The bug clung to the bumper by its powerful magnetic base.

Bolan continued on until he cleared the parked vehicles and made his way inside the diner, taking a booth where he could watch Quinn. The Executioner ordered coffee. Quinn had a large burger and extra fries. As he ate he kept up a constant chatter with the young woman behind the counter. Whatever he was saying kept her grinning.

They were in the diner for three-quarters of an hour. Bolan had sunk enough coffee to keep him awake until morning. When Quinn left, the soldier hung back until the panel truck exited the lot. Then he paid for his coffee and returned to his 4x4. The GPS tracking unit was compact and wide ranging. Bolan switched on the power and placed the device on the passenger seat. The unit went online and the satellite system aligned itself, displaying Quinn's line of travel on the highway. Bolan rolled out of the diner's parking lot and took his position about a half mile behind Quinn. It was down to the tracking unit now. All Bolan had to do was follow the pulsing dot on the screen.

Wherever Quinn went, the Executioner would not be far behind.

11

The thought crossed the Executioner's mind that there might be someone tracking *him,* following the signal sent out by his own vehicle. He understood the implications, accepted them and maintained his own quiet observations.

Light began to fade a couple of hours later. Bolan had kept his distance as the traffic around him lessened. Now there was nothing between Bolan and Quinn's panel truck. The soldier had extended his tailing distance to three-quarters of a mile.

Quinn turned off the main highway, and Bolan watched the marker on his GPS screen and picked up speed once his quarry was out of sight. As he approached the spot where Quinn had turned, Bolan slowed, saw the narrow side road and coasted onto it. It looked like nothing more than a dusty dirt road. In his rearview mirror Bolan saw dust raised by his own vehicle visible even in the twilight.

The GPS image showed that Quinn was far ahead. Bolan didn't worry. He could afford to let the man stay where he was. The dirt road was uneven, giving Bolan a bumpy ride. It would be worse for Quinn. Panel trucks were not designed for this kind of surface.

They traveled at least five miles before Quinn made another turn, drove another quarter mile, then came to an abrupt stop.

Bolan watched the tracker image. It was motionless now. He

monitored it for a few more minutes. Quinn had to have reached his destination.

A quarter mile from Quinn's spot Bolan turned off the dirt road and eased the 4x4 into a shallow dip in the landscape. The spot he had chosen was choked with scrub brush. Bolan reversed the Ford and backed as deep into the vegetation as he could, aware of the brush raking the sides of the truck.

Changing into combat gear, blacksuit and boots, Bolan armed himself, the big .44 Magnum Desert Eagle holstered on his right hip, the 9 mm Beretta 93-R snug in the shoulder rig. A Cold Steel Tanto knife was sheathed on his left side. The Executioner's longtime favorite and trusted 9 mm Uzi, fitted with a 32-round extended magazine, completed his ordnance. A lightweight combat harness carried extra magazines for his three weapons in closed pouches.

Bolan waited until full dark before he moved out. There was minimal light from a pale moon, which suited the Executioner just fine. He had already assumed that Quinn would most likely be waiting until dawn before he made contact with his incoming visitors. They would be delivering him something from over the border.

Speculation brought Bolan to the conclusion that Quinn had come to this lonely rendezvous to meet a crew from the Rojas Cartel. The cargo to be passed over would be a consignment of raw cocaine for delivery to one of Dembrow's factories. The valuable coke, cut and processed, would double in capacity. Its street value would soar each time it moved along the processing chain until the version that hit the streets would be far removed from the pure drug Quinn was about to pick up. That would mean little to the addicts clamoring for it. The last thing their drug-addled brains would tell them would be to watch what they put into their bodies. Some would sicken. Others would die in agony, reacting to the additions to the coke. None of that mattered to the merchants who peddled the stuff. Their one and only point of interest was the money they got from selling the drugs.

From the rich to the poor, the profit made from the coke Rojas was sending into America was all that mattered. The misery, the suffering, the addiction that fueled crime—it was all irrelevant to men like Marshal Dembrow and Benito Rojas. Every soldier in the Rojas Cartel was as guilty as the top men—Bolan had already marked them down for Executioner-style justice.

He took his time approaching Quinn's resting place. It turned out to be a large, tumbledown hut, long abandoned. Crouching in the sandy earth and scanning the hut, Bolan saw that Quinn had opened the sagging wooden doors and driven the panel truck inside, so that the only part of the vehicle still visible was the rear end. Bolan waited for an hour without seeing any movement before he closed in on the hut and slid along the passenger side of the truck. He checked inside the cab and saw Quinn stretched across the seats, a blanket pulled around him. Even through the closed windows of the truck Bolan could hear Quinn's ragged breathing as the man slept.

Backing off, Bolan made his way back to his own vantage point and settled down himself. He was going to have a long wait before Quinn's delivery arrived. That didn't worry Bolan. He could wait.

The Texas night might prove to be a chilly one—but the coming day was sizing up to be hot.

Executioner-style hot.

12

Choirboy hadn't spoken for a while. He was slumped in his seat and looked as if he might be asleep. Preacher knew differently and left his partner alone. He would say his piece when he had thought it out.

"You waiting on something?" Choirboy said eventually.

Preacher smiled. "I am, son."

"So?"

"I'm waiting for that guy to lead us away from town. Somewhere nice and private where we can deal with him without any pryin' eyes. There's too much business around here—people, cops and such. Hell, son, you should know that as much as I do. Sole reason we ain't never been tagged. Because we are careful. Damn, you forgot that?"

"No."

"You know what? I think you need a vacation. It comes to mind we been busy of late. A change of scene could be just what we need. We made enough cash to haul ourselves off somewhere and relax. What do you, say, son? Is it a good idea or what?"

Choirboy nodded. He sat upright, pointing at the tracker screen display. "He's moving again."

"He surely is."

They had been tracking the red Ford, following its progress

through Cooter's Crossing until it had veered off the main drag and picked up the highway that would take it across country.

"Where the hell is he going now?" Choirboy asked.

"South by the looks of it," Preacher said.

He eased the Lincoln out of the stream of traffic and cut across to pick up the highway. They were a good few miles behind the Ford, Preacher having stayed well back until he decided it was time to close in.

"Why's he been hanging around town the last couple of days?" Choirboy asked.

"Do I look like a psychic, son? We're getting paid to off the guy, not keep a check on his social calendar. Beauty of this here tracker is we can stay out of his shadow and still have him on our radar, so to speak."

They stayed on course, still holding back, tracking the red 4x4 into the dusk, observing as it swung off the highway. When they reached the turnoff, Preacher slowed, easing the heavy Lincoln onto soft, sandy soil. The Ford was well ahead now. Losing light made no difference. The signal blip still showed on the screen. Preacher brought the Lincoln to a crawl, feeling the vehicle losing some traction.

"Wish he'd stayed on the blacktop," Preacher muttered. "This old beauty ain't designed for desert travel."

"You don't say. Hell, I could walk faster than this."

Preacher cut the headlights, using only the side lights. The subdued illumination made it hard for him to stay on the trail proper, and a couple of times he veered to the side, the tires sinking into even softer soil.

"Damn."

Choirboy glanced at his partner. "I'm wondering if that bastard knows we're following him, and he's leading us off the highway so he can bust our asses."

"There are times, son, when you have a highly suspicious turn of mind."

"Well, excuse me for thinking outside the box."

"No offence," Preacher said. "You might have something. Never be afraid to look at a situation and extrapolate. Survival comes from looking at what might be, not always how it seems."

"Hey, he's stopped."

"He sure has."

"Meeting someone?"

Preacher stopped the car and turned off the engine.

"What?"

"It's too risky driving farther. We get dug in, this Cooper guy is going to be the one doing the killing. I got a feeling that 4x4 isn't going anywhere tonight, so we'll wait until morning. I'll take first watch and wake you in a few hours. If our friend moves, we'll be ready."

The Ford remained stationary through the night. Preacher watched the pulsing red signal on the screen, wondering just what Cooper was doing out here. He debated whether to call Dembrow, then decided against it. They were being paid to take out this guy. It wouldn't be professional to ring the client and ask him for advice. That wasn't how Preacher and Choirboy operated. They ran their business on a strictly self-regulating basis. You took a man's money and you did the job. You didn't expect him to bail you out if things became tricky.

He settled in the seat. One thing about the customized Lincoln. It was the most comfortable car he had ever ridden in. It was worth every penny he had paid to have the extras fitted. Come morning, once they completed their business with Cooper, Preacher and Choirboy would be that much closer to collecting the second half of their fee.

CHOIRBOY WAS ON WATCH as the day brightened around them, warmth starting to filter into the car. He stirred. Beside him Preacher still slept. A quick look at the monitor showed the Ford was still parked. Choirboy opened his door and stepped outside. He glanced at his watch—it was well after nine.

Choirboy roused Preacher.

"We need to move," he said.

Preacher started the car. He recalled the soft trail and eased the Lincoln forward slowly, feeling the tires grip, then slip a little.

He remained calm, easing them forward yard by yard until they hit a firmer stretch of the trail.

They both spotted the distant smudge of dark smoke staining the clean sky, then heard two dull explosions, spaced apart. Then more black smoke.

"What the hell is going on?" Preacher asked.

A little while on and Choirboy said, "Son of a bitch is on the move."

"Good."

"You might want to rethink that statement," Choirboy said. "He's heading right at us."

"Son, I think we might be in business. Time to break out the tools and go to work."

13

Quinn's company arrived around seven in the morning. They came in a black, personalized Humvee, its large tires churning up the sandy earth. The driver approached the hut, swinging around and reversing to the panel truck. Quinn had been up and waiting for them. The transfer took place without any formality of any kind, which left Bolan little time to make his move.

Aware his opportunity was limited, the soldier completed a second check of the numbers he would be going up against.

One man stood by the Humvee, ignoring the activity taking place up front. His subgun hung from his neck by a plaited leather strap. The big vehicle had been reversed up to the open doors of the hut.

Two was on a loose, roving patrol, and they obviously were not professionals. They were simply a pair of Latino hardmen, who would have had a drill sergeant tearing at his own buzz cut. Bolan didn't mind their laxity. It was going to make his job that much easier.

Quinn was busy taking the packs from Rojas's man and transferring them to the back of the panel truck. Bolan could hear a continuous rattle of talk as the men worked. They might as well have been delivering bread, rather than the poisonous product they were casually handling. Bolan didn't need to be any closer to recognize the thick, wrapped blocks of cocaine. He had seen similar packs many times before. Too many times.

Death and suffering were in every one of the blocks.

Bolan made a final check of the Beretta. He tapped the weapon, then holstered it and slipped from his cover to begin a circuitous approach that would bring him around to the roving guards. He used the tangled brush for cover, flitting from point-to-point silently, barely raising any dust as he moved. He rounded the far side of the shed, crouching in the deep shadow cast by the sun on the far end of the building and lay still as one of the guards slowly made another round.

Bolan let the guy walk by before he eased up off the dusty ground, the blade of the Tanto knife gleaming as it followed through in a continuous arc that ended when he drew the razor edge across the guy's exposed throat. The stricken guard struggled to contain the rush of hot blood flooding from the deep wound, too absorbed in his attempt to survive to even make an abortive attempt at yelling a warning. He fell to his knees, kicking against approaching death, unaware of Bolan's moving form as the Executioner stepped away from him.

The dead guard's partner was starting to turn, holding out a thin cigar he wanted his partner to light. The unexpected vision of Bolan standing at the corner of the hut froze him for a split second, then he dropped the cigar and went for his slung SMG. Bolan dropped to one knee, sliding the Beretta from its holster and tilting the muzzle at an angle. The cigar was still falling when Bolan stroked the 93-R's trigger. The Beretta emitted a soft whisper and sent a subsonic 9 mm slug on its brief journey. The slug struck the guard just above his right eye, the angle of the bullet coring in and up to cripple the guy's brain functions. It emerged from the top of his skull in a hot spurt of bone and flesh. The guard's head snapped back, and he went down in an ungainly sprawl.

Ahead of Bolan was the Humvee, with its relaxed guardian. The soldier circled again, coming up behind the guy. He flicked the Beretta's fire selector to 3-round burst and lined up on the back of the guard's skull. A simple squeeze on the trigger put a trio of 9 mm slugs on target. The guy pitched forward, his shoulder slamming against the hood of the Humvee as he slumped across it, blood leaking copiously from the ragged hole in his face where two of the slugs had emerged.

That left two—Quinn and the Latino guy helping him transfer the coke.

As Bolan crept around the far side of the Humvee, he saw the Mexican close the rear door of the vehicle. The guy abruptly turned, suspicion on his face when he realized none of his crew were in sight. He was opening his mouth to speak, reaching for the pistol holstered on his hip, when Bolan struck from where he crouched. The Tanto's blade went in under the guy's jaw, slicing in through soft flesh, grating on bone to penetrate through the jaw, spiking the guy's tongue. Bolan twisted on the handle, the blade cutting deep as he angled it clear. Bloody flesh parted easily. He turned the blade again, making a heavy left to right slash across the throat. The sentry dropped to his knees, blood spurting from his throat onto the dusty earth.

QUINN CLIMBED BACK out of the panel truck's cab where he had been helping himself to a swig from a bottle of Jack Daniel's whiskey. He was partial to the liquor and never left home without a quart bottle. He moved along the side of the truck, suddenly struck by the silence.

"Hey, Paco, you finished already?" he called. Silence greeted his request.

He swore.

Why did he always get the laziest sons of bitches assigned to help him?

Then he decided things were not quite right.

His right hand instinctively dropped to the pistol in a holster slung loosely around his waist. As his fingers touched the butt, a shadow flickered close on his right, too fast for him to fully register before he felt a left to right icy chill flash across his throat. As the cold sensation faded he experienced a burning in its place, then the sting of pain. His hand went to his throat in a natural reaction, and his fingers felt warm fluid. It was pulsing from a gaping wound in his throat, and Quinn knew it was blood, his own, now hot and sticky, surging over his fingers, spilling down his shirtfront in a rich cascade.

He saw, too, the figure dressed in midnight black, ice blue eyes staring at him without pity. A glittering steel blade in one raised hand. He knew now why Paco had not heeded his call. Quinn's life burst from him as his heart continued to pump, draining his strength, his resistance. He was on his knees, then facedown on the dirty floor of the hut, the only sound the rasping gasps coming from his throat as he desperately attempted to catch his ebbing breath. He slipped into death without even noticing someone removing his cell phone from his shirt pocket.

BOLAN LOOKED inside the Humvee and found a couple of reserve jerricans of gasoline in webbing straps against the side of the body and removed them. Climbing into the Humvee, he drove it clear of the hut. Then the soldier closed the panel truck doors and moved the vehicle from the hut and into a clear space. Bolan uncapped the gas cans and doused the Humvee and the hut. He placed the last half-can in the panel truck. He located a lighter on one of the dead guards and used it to ignite the gasoline. As flames engulfed the Humvee and the hut, Bolan drove the panel truck to where he had left his own vehicle. He transferred the cocaine from the truck to the rear of his Ford. While he worked, he heard the soft thump as the Humvee's gas tank blew, sending more flame and smoke skyward. When he had moved all the coke to the 4x4, Bolan moved his vehicle clear before he used the remaining gasoline to douse the panel truck and set it alight as well.

He drove away as the panel truck blazed and eventually heard the fuel tank explode, thick palls of black smoke rising to smear the Texas sky.

The Executioner had delivered his message to the cartel. It was a simple message.

Bolan wanted Rojas and Dembrow to know their business was under attack; to realize that they were no longer safe, because the

Executioner was not held back by laws that protected the guilty as well as the innocent.

Confusion and distraction would aid Bolan. He wanted his enemies off guard, allowing him the chance to move in closer and inflict whatever harm he could. It was a strategy Bolan had employed many times before and in most instances it gave him the results he wanted.

14

Preacher walked around to the rear of the Lincoln and opened the trunk. A large, flat aluminum case was inside, alongside the leather satchel holding the money Dembrow had given them. Choirboy smiled and stroked the satchel. Then he snapped the catches on the aluminum case and opened the lid. The case was lined with foam rubber, and had cutouts for various weapons.

"What do you want?" he called out.

Preacher had slipped off his suit jacket and laid it across the Lincoln's wide rear seat, placing his hat on top of it. When he joined Choirboy at the rear of the car, he leaned his hands against the rim of the trunk and studied the cased weapons.

"It's early in the day to make decisions," he said, "but she has to be done."

He reached in and picked out a Glock 21 .45ACP. It was one of Preacher's favorite weapons. He snapped in a magazine and worked the slide to arm the pistol. He pulled a leather belt and hip holster from the case, strapped it on and slid the Glock into the holster.

There was no hesitation when Choirboy hefted a Benelli M4 shotgun. He considered the combat weapon cool, with its sleek matte black configuration. The Super 90 looked to be a perfect fit in Choirboy's hands. He fed in six 12-gauge shells, picking up more to drop into a pocket.

"We're going to look foolish," Choirboy said, "if it ain't him. If it turns out to be a Border Patrol cruiser."

"Trust me, son, it's him." Preacher helped himself to an M-16 A-4 rifle. "Come to daddy."

The M-16 was the American military's weapon of choice. Since its inception, the M-16 assault rifle had regenerated through various updates until the M-16 A-4 model. Chambered in 5.56 mm, taking a 30-round magazine, the weapon was capable of 3-round bursts, or single shot. Since the time he had been handed his first model, Preacher had taken to the rifle with a passion. He had owned and used different incarnations, but as far as he was concerned it was the M-16. Each new version became his challenge of the moment. He stripped it down, worked on every aspect of its makeup until he had the rifle tuned to perfection. He understood it, knew its limits and made it speak for him.

And he never, ever allowed anyone to touch his rifle.

Not even Choirboy—though they shared everything else they owned. Only one man had ignored the warnings and had been handling the M-16 when Preacher had walked in on him.

No one spoke, not even Preacher. He simply took the rifle from the guy's hands and placed it back in its case. Everyone figured that was an end to it—except Choirboy. He had seen the empty expression in Preacher's eyes, and he knew the worst was to come.

Nothing happened for a few days, and then word got around that the guy who had handled Preacher's rifle had been found at the roadside out of town screaming for help because someone had skewered his eyes out and severed both his hands.

The matter was never brought up. No one would talk about it, or offer an explanation. It was as if the incident had never occurred. Nobody knew anything.

Except Choirboy.

And he wasn't talking either.

Preacher picked up a 30-round magazine for the M-16 A-4. He tapped it against the Lincoln's trunk edge, then clicked it into the rifle. Working the cocking lever, Preacher walked to the front of the Lincoln and leaned against the fender.

"How we going to do this?" Choirboy asked.

"Seeing as how we're in the middle of nowhere and I don't see any appreciable cover, son, there ain't no way to go but direct."

"He ain't about to drive right up and let us shoot him," Choirboy pointed out.

"True enough."

Preacher checked the air again, nodding to himself as he established the lack of breeze. That in itself was unusual. More often than not there was a noticeable degree of air movement, sometimes quite strong. But this day, at least for the moment, the warming Texas air was motionless. Preacher hoped it would remain so.

Choirboy had taken a pair of binoculars from the glove box of the car, and he was scanning the rutted trail. He scanned the landscape, seeing nothing of interest—only the wide Texas emptiness.

"Nothing there," he said, then swept the glasses back as he detected movement. "Wait. Wait. Son of a bitch, there he is. See his dust? You see it?"

"Hell, yes, I see it, son. And he's coming right this way."

Preacher shouldered the M-16 A-4, bracing himself close to the fender of the car. The red Ford had eased over the top of a slope in the trail and was clean in his sights. He had already calculated the vehicle was within range—and if it was in range Preacher could hit it.

BOLAN FELT the 4x4 roll over the lip of the slope. He immediately spotted the vehicle blocking the trail, and saw the two men beside it. One peered through binoculars while the other leveled a rifle in the Executioner's direction.

He remembered his suspicions of being followed. Being right about that was no comfort to him. It snapped him back from his moment of weariness following his long night watch over Walt Quinn.

You let things slide there. Expected too much. And now you might have to pay the price, he thought.

The seconds raced by, Bolan's mind in a whirl of mental activity as he sought a solution to what was happening.

There was nowhere to run. No cover of any kind, just flat emptiness.

He needed to exit the Ford, get flat down on the ground where he would present a lesser target.

Bolan snatched up the Uzi from the seat beside him. The gun was fully loaded. As his fingers closed around the weapon, he stomped on the brake and brought the 4x4 to a crawl.

He worked the door handle. Rolling to the left, he let his shoulder slam against the door panel and it flew open. Bolan launched himself off the seat.

As he started to fall, he heard the chunk of a bullet strike the windshield, then slap against the back of the driver's seat. He hit the dusty ground, grunting at the impact, moving instantly. He crawled toward the rear of the 4x4, kicking up clouds of dust. He knew he was marking his position, but right then he didn't give a damn. His prime intention was to reach cover, any cover, before being killed.

A second shot threw a slug into the ground just short of his scrabbling feet. A third clipped the heel of his combat boot, wrenching his foot to one side.

"I MISSED THE MOTHER," Preacher yelled. "Jesus, I don't miss."

"Well, hell, you did this time."

Preacher broke away from the front of the Lincoln, moving fast as he closed on the truck. The 4x4 was still creeping forward slowly, under its own power.

"Go around," Preacher yelled at his partner. "Go around, son, this bastard ain't getting free and clear."

Choirboy began a wide circle, the Benelli gripped tight against his side as he ran. The soft sand underfoot slowed him as it tugged at his boots. He could see the 4x4 side-on now, the wheels still turning slowly as the vehicle maintained some motion.

Choirboy crouched and tried to peer underneath the vehicle.

Where the hell was the guy?

Choirboy couldn't see him at the rear of the Ford, or anywhere else. He had to be close, because there was no way he could have moved clear. There wasn't a damn place to hide.

The man would have to be lower than a snake's belly to conceal himself out here.

"Shit."

Realization hit hard. The bastard hadn't run. He was flat down on the ground. Choirboy turned, seeking his partner to warn him.

In trying to alert Preacher, Choirboy failed to see Bolan rise to his knees, coming up out of the shallow depression he had dropped into. The Uzi rose with him, the muzzle tracking in. The full-auto burst spit 9 mm slugs into Choirboy's torso, kicking out spurts of blood as they struck. Choirboy gave a startled scream as he was hit. Pain was a new thing to him—usually he was inflicting it on others. Now he was the one twisting in agony, his body alive with terrible pain. He felt himself topple backward, the Benelli exploding with sound as his finger jerked back against the trigger.

Bolan heard the crackle of returned fire from the first shooter. Dirt geysered into the air around him. The shooter was firing on the move, not pausing to aim. Bolan recognized the hard sound of an M-16.

That meant a 30-round magazine.

Bolan caught a flicker of movement as the shooter ran behind the bulk of the truck, which was between them both now.

Damn.

The last thing the soldier wanted was some drawn out cat-and-mouse game.

Bolan crouched and flattened against the rear wheel of the 4x4. He bent to peer beneath the vehicle and saw his opponent's lower legs and boots. He angled the muzzle of the Uzi around and triggered a burst that sheared into the dirt inches away as the guy shifted position. He was moving around the rear of the 4x4.

Bracing one foot against the tire, Bolan kicked back, shoving himself away from the Ford and falling on his back, the Uzi searching for its target.

Preacher stepped into view, his finger already on the trigger of the M-16. His guess that Bolan would still be hugging the bulk of the 4x4 was wrong. His misjudgment left him off guard, and Bolan stitched him with a sustained burst that cleared the Uzi's magazine.

The multiple hits staggered Preacher. Flesh and bone erupted from his back, blowing out with stunning force. Preacher worked the trigger of the rifle, feeling it jerk as it fired. He felt the weapon slipping from his fingers. His gaze dropped, and he saw the bloody mess soaking his shirt. As he fell, he caught a glimpse of Choirboy's equally bloody form on the ground yards away.

"He killed us, son," he whispered before he fell facedown on the ground.

On his feet, Bolan moved to the Ford. He dropped the spent Uzi on the seat, leaning in to switch off the idling engine. He leaned against the side of the 4x4, pressing a hand to the spot in his side where one of the assassin's bullets had burned across his skin. He slipped the Beretta from its shoulder holster and crossed to where the man lay. He checked the killer's pulse, satisfying himself that the guy was dead, then he walked across to where the other man lay.

Choirboy lay bloody and still, except for his eyes. They stared up at Bolan. Choirboy's bloody lips moved slowly as he formed words.

"Preacher dead?"

Bolan nodded.

"At least you done saved Dembrow from having to pay the rest of his fee."

"He put out the contract on me?"

"Dembrow ain't the sort who takes kindly to being messed with. You kind of upset him killing his boys."

"He's going to have to get used to that."

Choirboy made a weak smile. "I do believe you mean it."

"You kill Don Manners?"

"What the hell," Choirboy said. "Ain't as if I'm walking away from this. Yeah. Preacher and me done for him."

Choirboy saw the chill message in Bolan's eyes and as he took his last breath, he could only think that Dembrow better watch his back.

15

Bolan stood beside the Ford. The tracking device in the vehicle had made it possible for Preacher and Choirboy to locate him. It had come that close. Time to make a change. He reached a decision, climbed into the 4x4 and drove to where the big Lincoln sat. He cleared the drugs from the Ford and stacked them in the Continental's spacious trunk, where he also placed his weapons bag. Bolan inspected the aluminum case of weapons found in the Lincoln and took the ammunition that would feed his own weapons, then dumped the case on the ground. The leather satchel in the trunk yielded a substantial amount of cash. The hit team's payment from Dembrow? Bolan left the satchel where it was.

Before he did anything else Bolan stripped out of his combat gear and changed back into civilian clothing. There was a small first-aid box clipped to the side of the Lincoln's trunk. He cleaned the burn mark on his side and placed an adhesive bandage over it, then closed and locked the trunk. His Beretta went into the Lincoln's glove box. As he went to climb into the vehicle, Bolan saw the coat and hat on the rear seat. He opened the door and threw the garments out of the car.

Bolan started the Lincoln, feeling the surge of power from the big engine. Aware of how the big cruiser sat low against the trail, he turned the car carefully, not wanting it to bog down. He kept the car in the center of the trail as he drove. The air-conditioning unit pumped out a cool draft that felt good against his face.

The Lincoln had been customized with extras that included a fitted sat phone. He tapped a number that would be routed to Stony Man Farm and listened to the contact being made over the inset speakers.

Barbara Price's calm voice was a welcome relief.

"Are the eyes of Texas still upon you?" she asked.

"Keeping me busy."

"Nice to hear. On that theme I have updates for you following on from what Hal said. Bear found out some details on the perps at the diner. They were definitely associated with Marshal Dembrow. And they were local street soldiers. Low on the ladder."

"But at least we know who they collected their blood money from."

Bolan's thoughts dwelled again on Pilar Trujillo, a beautiful young woman who had been drawn into the hungry maw of evil through no fault of her own. And she had paid the ultimate price—cut down by the lowlifes who took their orders from Marshal Dembrow. It was an unnecessary death through association and an old story Bolan had heard so many times before. The darkness reached out and touched any who stepped within range. There was no distinction between good or bad. Collateral damage—a cold, oblique reference that encompassed those who suffered through the deliberate actions of others. Bolan could never accept the concept as ever being justified.

"You still there?" Price asked.

"I'm here. Message for the head man," Bolan said. "Tell him I hit one of the cartel deliveries today—cargo from Mexico to the local agent. Rojas to Dembrow. Walt Quinn was there to pick up the consignment. It was his last collection ever. The delivery team is down, too, and I have the consignment in the trunk of my car. Enough coke to probably fund the Farm for the next couple of years, if we were into that."

"Nice score, Striker. What happens to the coke?"

"I'm going to use it as bait to draw in both parties. Rojas and

Dembrow are going to want it back. If I can make it work, they'll be fighting each other over it."

"I like the sound of that. Take care, Striker, these are nasty people."

"I know," Bolan said. "One more thing. You can relay a message for me to the DEA, however you want to send it. Tell them the hit team who took out Don Manners has been paid in full. They won't be taking on any more contracts. They were bankrolled by Marshal Dembrow. The only name I got was Preacher. They might want to check it out."

"Leave that with me," Price replied. "We have a cell phone number for Tomas Trujillo. It came from Manners via Pilar." The mission controller read out the number. "Is that going to be a help?"

"Definitely. Thanks."

16

Bolan drove back to his hotel. He parked the Lincoln in a corner of the hotel's basement garage. His weapons were back in the carry-all he carried with him back to his room. Before settling in, Bolan stashed the bag in the large closet, then took the time to have a shower before he dressed in fresh clothing.

He called room service and ordered food and coffee. While he waited, he contacted Stony Man Farm again and asked for Kurtzman.

"I need an empty building where I can arrange for a meet. Somewhere out of town and well away from locals. I don't want the chance of any civilians getting hurt."

"I'll work on it and get back to you," Kurtzman said.

"Make it fast. I need to set this up ASAP."

Bolan's room-service order arrived a short time later and he realized how hungry he was. He had finished his meal and was downing a second cup of coffee when his cell phone rang. It was Kurtzman.

"The Northwest Meat-Packing Plant stands on its own grounds. It's been closed down for four years and it's supposed to be under development, but no takers so far. The place is pretty well derelict. No other businesses are close by. Railway tracks run alongside the plant, and no one wanted to be near the place when it was up and running, so it's isolated. I'll send you a text with directions. Is that what you're looking for?"

"Exactly what I'm looking for. *Gracias.*"

"Hey, talking the lingo now."

Bolan ended the call. He drained his coffee, picked up his phone again and dialed in the phone number Price had supplied.

It rang out for a long time before it was answered.

"¿Quién habla?"

"A friend who can help Benito Rojas get back his missing cargo," Bolan said.

"¿Qué?" The language changed abruptly. "Who the fuck are you? And what is this missing cargo you are talking about?" A pause, then, "How did you get my fucking number?"

"Maybe I'm a fan, Trujillo. Tomas Trujillo, isn't it?"

"You screwing me around?"

"Do some checking. Your delivery crew met with Walt Quinn to hand over a coke stack. They drove a black, customized Humvee. Quinn was waiting for them. Someone else was waiting for the meet to take place. They took out your crew and Quinn, and made off with the cargo. It's easy enough for you to check out."

"Hombre, you shouldn't play fucking games."

"This is no game. I don't give a damn if you haven't the time to listen. But I do know Rojas is not going to be a happy man if you lose him the chance to take back his coke." Bolan could almost feel the tension as Trujillo considered his options. "Hey, I don't have all day."

"Espere un momento."

Bolan picked up voices in the background. There was a rattle as the cell phone was transferred from one hand to another. A different voice came on the line.

"What shit is this you are giving me?"

"If you're Benito Rojas, you'll know what I'm talking about when you try to contact your delivery crew. So listen. I know about your cargo going missing. You want it back, I'll tell you where it will be the day after tomorrow."

"So you say. How do I know this is not a trick?"

"Figure it out, *hombre*. I know who took it and where it is. I could take the stuff myself and make my own deal if I felt inclined. But I understand you're a big man. Anyone who decided to screw you over wouldn't live long enough to spend the money. So I figure I'd give you back your shit, and maybe you'll do me a favor and toss me some commission."

Rojas laughed. "I have to admire your initiative."

"I'm not looking for a pat on the back. Just a way to turn what I know into hard cash. Are you interested?"

"That missing cargo is worth a great deal. A very great deal. Getting my hands on it is important to me."

"Then listen. The day after tomorrow at eight o'clock. The cargo will be waiting for pickup by an interested party at the old Northwest Meat-Packing Plant outside Cooter's Crossing. You know it?"

"*Sí.*"

"Come in by the east gate. Main shed. Your cargo will be there. Send your people to pick it up. The interested party will be there, too, so tell your crew to watch their backs. And don't move any earlier. You'll be watched. Break the rules, the game is off."

"Do not fool with me," Rojas said. "If this is not what you say…"

"It wasn't me who hijacked your shipment, Rojas. Maybe this is a way to find out who did."

"How will I contact you?"

"No problem, Señor Rojas. I have this number, so I can call you."

BOLAN'S SECOND CALL ran along the same lines, except that he spoke directly to Marshal Dembrow. The American was in a no-nonsense mood.

"You fucking with me, boy? Do you have my consignment?"

"Your drugs? I don't have them, but I know where they'll be day after tomorrow—waiting for pickup by people who made an offer. It seems to me, Dembrow, that your pickup guy and Rojas's crew were a little careless letting that coke get hijacked and themselves wiped out. Never would have figured Walt Quinn letting something like that happen. Always saw Walt as sharper than that."

"Fuck the reminiscences. How do you get off knowing where my stuff is?"

"You don't expect me to give up my sources," Bolan said. "Let's just say I keep my ears open and my head down. I'm in this for a kickback. You get your hands on the coke, I get a finder's fee. That's all. You interested?"

"Maybe."

"Maybe! Hell, Dembrow, I can hear you foaming at the mouth from here. If I do this for you, I expect to be paid."

"Where and when?"

"Day after tomorrow. The Northwest Meat-Packing Plant, Cooter's Crossing. The place was closed down years ago, so you shouldn't be disturbed. Eight o'clock. West gate. The coke will be inside the main shed. Just watch out for the buyer's crew. If anyone moves in before the deadline, the deal's off and the coke gets reduced to ashes. Take it from me, you don't want to screw around with these people. That's it, Dembrow. Your choice."

Bolan cut the call and switched off his phone.

He had set the deal in motion.

All he could do now was sit back and see if both parties took the bait.

17

Bolan parked the Lincoln and went EVA. He was on the eastern perimeter of the packing plant, the railway tracks some distance behind him. He had scouted the area earlier in the day, finding a narrow, disused road that paralleled the sagging fence of the plant. On the other side rusted holding pens stretched almost all the way to the large, empty main packing shed. Other smaller huts dotted the site, all of them in disrepair. There had once been a spur line that allowed cattle cars to roll in close to the pens, but the tracks had rusted and were overgrown with grass and weeds. The whole area reeked of desolation and disuse. Loose corrugated steel sheets rattled in the dry wind blowing in from the wide land beyond Cooter's Crossing.

Crouching just inside the fence, Bolan scanned the area. It was just after four in the morning, dark and chilly. He knew without having yet seen them that there were others at the site. One of the two principals—he didn't know which—had sent in an advance team. Bolan had spotted a dark-colored car parked on the far side of the site, behind a couple of old railcars. His recon had paid off. Checking the car, he touched the hood. It was still warm, and he could hear the soft pinging coming from the cooling engine.

In the shadows Bolan studied the long packing shed. Dark figures flitted through a patch of moonlight. He smiled without humor. His senses had warned him that someone would try to gain the advantage. True to form the drug traffickers revealed their nature. They were unable to act in any other way than by being duplicitous, by going against any promise made, no matter how nebulous.

Fine by me, Bolan decided. You want to play—let's do it by my rules.

He crouch-walked, his blacksuited figure blending with the night shadows. Bolan was in his element, using the darkness as a partner, letting it conceal his movements as he neared the packing shed.

The Beretta 93-R was in its shoulder rig. His only other weapon was the Cold Steel Tanto knife, the silky smooth blade hungry for blood.

He counted his quarry as he moved back and forth, silent, probing the shadows.

The three hardmen were speaking Spanish in muted voices.

Inside the packing shed, the dark was interrupted by pale swaths of moonlight sliding in through gaps in the roof and walls. The main area empty, the sides of the building stacked with debris, tangled metalwork and discarded wooden frames.

The trio, each carrying an SMG, moved back and forth. Their voices rose as they realized there was nothing to see. Whatever they might have expected didn't appear to exist.

One man produced a cell phone and punched in a number. He spoke rapidly. Bolan picked up the name Rojas. The man changed his tone, his agitation turned to deference as he spoke to his employer. Then he became apologetic. After a muttered farewell he snapped the phone shut and spoke to his companions.

Bolan picked up some of the conversation.

"What do we do?"

"Look again, he orders."

A silence.

Then, "So we look again."

The three split up. One started to check the debris inside the building. The others turned and took opposite exits from the plant.

Bolan watched the inside man. He was quietly muttering to himself as he inspected the debris, moving across the shed in Bolan's direction. The big American sank deeper into cover as the Mexican trafficker neared his position. The Executioner turned the Tanto cutting edge up, and as the guy stepped within touching distance, Bolan struck. The keen steel went in hard, up to the hilt, penetrating the pumping heart and tore it apart. Bolan turned his wrist, while his free hand reached up to catch hold of the man's neck, pulling him down. The severed heart slowed, faltered, and the weakening trafficker fell to his knees. The only sound he uttered was a long release of air from his open mouth. The soldier lowered the still body to the floor, withdrawing the blade and sheathing it after wiping off the blood.

Turning quickly, Bolan slipped the 93-R from its holster and went after the remaining members of the team.

He located the first man, who stood only feet away from the exit door, his head moving back and forth as he searched without enthusiasm. Bolan issued a silenced burst to the back of the man's skull, pitching the guy facedown on the ground.

The lone survivor was around the far side of the shed, striding toward a stack of rusting metal drums. He stopped and turned, his move fast and done with purpose. Bolan assumed he had heard his approach. The guy brought his SMG around as he turned, the muzzle searching. Bolan dropped to a crouch, firing without hesitation, and placed the 3-round burst into the man's chest. The Mexican dropped, his pulverized heart beating for a few more seconds before it shut down.

Bolan dragged each body through the shadows, rolling them into an open storm culvert at the side of the site. He moved debris and covered the bodies. The Executioner then drove the trio's car onto the unused, overgrown road where he had parked the Lincoln.

Moments later Bolan brought the Lincoln to the packing shed where he unloaded the cocaine and stacked it on a wooden pallet in the center of the floor. Then he returned the Lincoln to its concealed spot on the side road. By the time he had completed his endeavors, it was coming up to six o'clock and the dawn was emerging from the darkness. Light broke through even as Bolan made his way inside the packing shed and worked his way into the tangle of debris lining one wall. He chose a spot where the corrugated side panels were loose, offering him an exit from the building once the action started.

Bolan settled down to wait. He drew a plastic bottle of water from a side pocket of the blacksuit and took a sip.

He was as ready as he ever could be.

TWO MINUTES before eight o'clock, Bolan heard the sound of vehicles approaching from the east and west sides of the site. Tires slid on the dirt as the vehicles came to a stop. Doors slammed.

Bolan heard the tall doors being pulled open.

He picked up the sound of footsteps and the murmur of voices as the separate groups advanced into the gloom of the building.

Bolan waited until everyone was inside the large shed before he stirred the pot. From his concealed position midway along the structure, he could make out the dark mass of each group. He didn't wait any longer, knowing that recognition could occur at any moment. Bolan raised his Uzi and threw a swift burst in the direction of one group, then brought the muzzle around and fired a second burst at the other.

The shots echoed with a tinny sound inside the abandoned meat-packing shed. Then came startled yells in Spanish and English. The shouting continued as orders were issued in angry tones, followed by the scattering of feet, and the inevitable rattle of return fire.

Bolan backed away, using the debris to cover his retreat. He slid from the building through the gap in the corrugated sheeting. He emerged into the daylight, briefly shielding his eyes from the harsh glare of the sun, and stepped into the cover offered by the stacked metal drums and containers. Reaching the end of the stack, Bolan withdrew the tarp-wrapped bundle he had stashed there—the M-203 grenade launcher and the satchel of HE rounds from his weapons bag. Bolan loaded the first grenade, then moved on along the side of the building.

He could still hear sporadic firing from inside the shed. It wouldn't continue for much longer. The soldier increased his pace, crouching, his targets ahead of him at the east end of the packing shed. He spotted the parked 4x4s, top of the line models. It was an expensive collection of vehicles. Bolan sighted in and launched the first grenade. He was reloading even as the grenade hit and detonated, the target erupting in a blinding flash, followed by the gritty slam of the explosion. Shards of once pristine metal flew in all direction; fire and smoke rose from the shattered hulk of the vehicle. Bolan laid down two more grenades in quick succession, the dull thump of the explosions filling the hot air. In a matter of seconds he had reduced the parked vehicles to blazing wrecks, gutted and blackened. Debris rained back to earth.

Bolan turned away, moving to the west end of the shed where he found more 4x4s, plus a gleaming Lexus in burnished silver. He aimed the M-203 at the Lexus and fired, the grenade's curving trajectory ending when it slammed into the midsection of the luxury car. The Lexus blew apart in a burst of flame and smoke as armed men burst from the shed. The force of the blast sent them staggering. Bolan didn't allow them time to recover. He loaded and fired two more grenades, taking out the rest of the vehicles and leaving the stunned enemy staring at thousands of dollars going up in smoke. Bolan scattered them with bursts from the M-16, 5.56 mm slugs catching unprotected bodies.

His exercise completed, Bolan eased away from the scene. There was no more he could achieve here. His next move would be the phone calls to Rojas and Dembrow to add a little suspicion to the brew.

The harsh command that reached his ears made Bolan pause. As he turned around he saw a thin, sallow-faced individual step out from behind a stack of wooden pallets, an autopistol in his left hand.

"Who the fuck are you?" the guy asked, his accent unmistakably American. His pale eyes searched Bolan's figure and took in the ordnance he wore. The man was clad in a crumpled suit, blood spattering the expensive material. His receding dark hair exposed a broad, glistening forehead. He stepped closer to Bolan, his gaze on the weaponry Bolan wore. He pointed his right hand at the M-16, and Bolan lowered the weapon.

"You the son of a bitch who shot everything up back there?"

"I guess I helped a little."

The autopistol jerked. "So who do you work for?"

"Department of Health and Sanitation. The old meat plant needed cleaning out."

"The fuck you say."

"One thing you should know. I never lie. That shed was full of vermin that had to be eradicated."

The implication was not lost on the guy—the soldier had to give him credit for that—and his sallow complexion flushed with righteous anger. Bolan saw his trigger finger tense and knew he had seconds to react. He dropped to the ground in the split second it took for the guy to pull the trigger, heard the sharp crack of the shot as the 9 mm slug passed over his head. Bolan hit the dusty ground, rolling and driving his legs around in a hard sweep. He caught the startled thug just above the ankles and watched him fall. Before his adversary hit the ground, Bolan had slipped the Cold Steel Tanto knife from its sheath. Using his left hand, he pushed himself off the ground, dropping half across the guy's body.

The glittering blade made two swift cuts. The first slashed across the man's left wrist, biting deep and severing tendons and veins. His autopistol dropped from numbed fingers. A rising scream was cut off as the Tanto's second slash cut deep into the guy's neck, just below the right ear, sliding around and across his throat. The sound that emanated from the stricken man was little more than a wet gurgle. He was still bleeding out as Bolan regained his feet, picked up the grenade launcher and moved quickly from the scene of devastation.

Behind him, thick smoke coiled into the cloudless Texas sky. The shooting had ceased altogether by then, but the crackling and popping from burning vehicles could still be heard, mingling with the confused and angry shouts coming from the dazed survivors.

Bolan powered across the compound, weaving in and out of

the cattle pens. He ducked through the fence and headed for the Lincoln. The Executioner reached his concealed vehicle. He opened the trunk and threw his M-16 and the grenade satchel inside. He slid behind the wheel and fired up the engine, swinging the car around and driving away in a long sweep that took him well clear of the site. No shots were fired in his direction. Bolan imagined that both groups would have identified themselves by now and would be busy trying to figure out who had been trying to screw whom. He stopped once to strip off his equipment and change back into civilian clothing. The battle gear went into the canvas bag in the rear of the truck.

Bolan used his smartphone to call 911. When his call was answered he spoke.

"Northwest Meat-Packing Plant. Shots were fired and people are hurt. If you move fast, you might find a big cocaine haul there."

He finished the call and kept driving. A couple of minutes later he heard sirens wailing, moving in from different directions. A police cruiser sped past, siren howling and the light bar blazing.

Bolan pulled in at the first truck stop he saw. Inside he chose a booth where he could see the road, ordered coffee and took out the cell phone he had acquired.

He saw more police cruisers go by, as well as a fire truck and an ambulance.

Bolan waited as his coffee was placed in front of him, then hit the number he had for Dembrow. He heard the number connect and ring.

"What?" someone demanded. The tone was harsh.

"You're not Dembrow," Bolan said.

"No, I ain't Dembrow. And who the fuck are you?"

"He'll know. Just put him on."

Bolan heard the guy suck in a sharp breath, then turn aside to speak away from the phone. Subdued voices, followed by someone snatching the phone from the first guy.

"Make it fast. I ain't too happy the way things turned out."

"The way things turned out, Dembrow?"

"Mr. Dembrow to you."

"Dembrow, you have to earn respect before it's returned."

"Listen, ass wipe, say what you have to else I'm liable to have your balls torn off and force-fed back to you," Dembrow taunted.

"Interesting concept. Useless, though, because we've never met and you don't know who I am," Bolan said.

"Okay, boy, we've both proved we're hard-asses, can we get to the sharp end?"

"Looks to me your buddy Rojas set up your guys at the packing plant. Word coming out of Old Mexico has him working to cut you out of the game. Since you let that undercover agent, Manners, inside your organization, Rojas doesn't see you as a long-term partner anymore."

Dembrow's pause was long enough for Bolan to figure he had taken the bait. Maybe only tentatively and he hadn't bitten down on the hook, but the silence told Bolan the man was considering.

"Why the hell should I believe anything you say? You put me on to the meet and next thing my guys are being shot at. The whole thing was a damn massacre."

"That's one of today's ills," Bolan said. "People don't trust anymore. They take a genuine offer and start looking for the angles."

"I didn't just come over the border with a bunch of wetbacks. You talked about angles—you must have one."

"Just one American to another. I see you have an upcoming problem so I thought I'd warn you. I wouldn't want to see you backstabbed by a damn Mex pusher."

Dembrow's harsh laugh rattled down the phone. "I'd love to see Rojas's face if you quoted that line to him. Hell, the guy runs the biggest cartel in Mexico."

"Maybe he wants it all to himself. Cut out the local connection and deal his own cards. Go figure."

Bolan cut the call.

"Have a nice day, Mr. Dembrow."

Bolan would have been aware of something out of place if his door had been unlocked. But he inserted his key card, heard the click as the lock released and pushed the door open.

The warning came too late. The sight of his clothing scattered across the bed alerted him, but he had already taken a step forward, and in that moment he caught the shadows on either side. Rough hands grabbed at his clothing, and he was propelled across the carpeted floor. He heard the rush of someone closing in. The solid slam of a hard blow across the back of his neck weakened him and Bolan dropped to his knees. A figure loomed over him, the stubby shape of a leather sap slashed down and delivered a stunning blow to the side of his skull, then a hard shoe drove into his side. The impact drove the breath from his body. More blows followed, not giving Bolan a chance to retaliate until he was flipped onto his back.

One of his attackers bent to strike again and this time Bolan reacted, his right foot kicking out and up. The sole of his shoe caught the guy in the face and he staggered back, moaning as he put his hands to his smashed nose.

"Son of a bitch broke my nose," he said.

"The hell with that," someone else said. "Get the bastard under control."

The demand spurred on Bolan's attackers and they closed on

him with a vengeance, feet and hands beating him into reluctant submission.

Bolan tried to ignore the frenzied attack, but even his resistance wavered and when his battered form was dragged to a kneeling position he was still fighting back. Then a savage blow to the back of his skull took away the final shreds of his ability to resist. A second blow started to bring down the blackness. In the final seconds before it enveloped him, Bolan saw, with startling clarity, a uniformed figure standing against the room's far wall.

It was Sam, the hotel bellman, watching Bolan with rabid interest, a crooked smile on his lips.

Then the blackness reached out and drew Bolan into its embrace. Everything shut down around him.

HE LAY STILL after he came to. He was in a world of pain, but it was bearable, and his ears attuned to what was around him. Extraneous sounds filtered through—movement, muted voices, the scrape of shoe leather on the hard concrete floor where he was lying.

"I reckon the bastard is awake. Just lying there listening to us."

"You think so?" This was an older voice, rough and nasal. "So get the mother on his feet and in the fuckin' chair."

Footsteps closed in on where Bolan lay. Hands grasped his clothing, and he was dragged across the floor and thrust onto a hard-backed chair. Bolan still needed time for his senses to realign themselves, so he stayed still.

"Ain't so damn smart now, Cooper. Figured you could come down here and make fools of us country boys? Like that last Fed tried. Hell, boy, you figure we're that dumb?"

The voice was harsh, with a low, raspy tone, and it had a mean edge to it.

The guy stood in front of Bolan. He wore a rumpled suit, and his shirt clung damply to his stocky body. He had a flat, loose-fleshed face with small, angry eyes, and his hair was thin and sandy, showing an expanse of wrinkled scalp. He was kneading the thick fingers of his big hands. Bolan recognized him from the downloaded images Stony Man had sent him.

Chris Malloy. Local deputy. A man on the take.

"Nothing to say, huh? You make this huge mess and now that we caught you there isn't a word?"

"For you, Malloy? Oh, I've got words. But I'll save them for the right time."

Malloy showed surprise at Bolan recognizing him. It made him miss a beat.

"This is no place for you to be making threats," he said.

Bolan raised his head. "No threats, Malloy. Your secret is out. If you want, I can quote you on the illegal bank deposits. All the payoffs you've had from Dembrow. And don't try going for it. The accounts have been blocked. Your money is ours now."

Malloy hit him, a deliberate punch that pushed Bolan's head back, blood spurting from a torn lip. The man was unnerved. He stared at Bolan, his face ashen.

"You can't touch me," he said, his conviction weak.

Bolan had touched a nerve, and Malloy was having difficulty handling the revelation. He turned away from Bolan and had hurried words with his two helpers. Malloy left the room, the slope of his shoulders telling Bolan the corrupt cop was worried.

A third figure materialized from behind Bolan. It was Sam the bellman. He moved so that he was behind the other men. It was clear he got some kind of excitement from watching Bolan being manhandled. He still had that odd smile on his face, the flesh glistening with an oily sheen. He kept clenching and unclenching his fists as he watched.

"What's the problem, Sam?" Bolan asked. "Not a big enough tip, so you sold me to the local goon squad?"

Sam's sick smile widened.

"This isn't negotiable, by the way," one of the men said. He was tall and lean, his dark hair cut close to his skull. "You let us in on what you're doing here so we can cover our asses, then you die. Or you get a lot of pain and you still die."

"I hope the bastard plays stubborn," the second guy said. He was the one Bolan had kicked. His nose was pushed out of line, still bloody, and there was no doubt he was hurting. Where the first man was lean, this one had the build of a wrestler, with wide shoulders and a barrel chest. He glared at Bolan with barely controlled rage. "I knew those guys who were killed at the shoot-out. I want to hurt the fucker."

"Ease off, Brad, we've got time."

Bolan noticed now that the lean guy was holding the 93-R. He carried it in his left hand. Taking a moment, Bolan checked out the rest of the room. No window. A strong light behind a wire cover filled the room with a bright glare. Apart from the chair Bolan occupied, there was no other furniture in the room. Brick walls and a concrete floor. In one corner of the room Bolan recognized his weapons bag. Next to it was the leather satchel with the money he had taken from the trunk of the Lincoln.

The skinny guy noticed Bolan's interest in the bags.

"You travel hard," he said. "Enough firepower to raise all hell. So what is that all about?"

"I like to cover all eventualities."

"Fuck, yeah. Well, it doesn't look like standard issue. What are you, pal, a salesman for Weapons Are Us? And what's with the black Ninja outfit?"

"Maybe I just like dressing up."

"Come on, Danny, let me ask the questions," Brad said. He was getting restless, constantly dabbing at his nose with a bloody, wadded up towel. "I'll get you answers."

He pushed forward, edging his partner aside.

Bolan came up off the chair, a blur of motion as he went directly for Danny and the Beretta. He slammed into the guy, reaching for the pistol, closing his hand over the 93-R's bulk and twisting. He drove the point of his left elbow up at Danny's throat full-on and heard the crunch of cartilage. Danny choked. The Beretta came into Bolan's hand and he clasped the butt, finger through the trigger guard.

"Mother..." Brad yelled and swung toward Bolan.

The Beretta arced around. Bolan stroked the trigger and the pistol chugged out a triburst that impacted against the side of Brad's skull. The three 9 mm slugs cored in through the bone, tearing at the mass of the brain and blew out the opposite side. Brad stumbled. Coordination went and he fell heavily. Blood started to spread out from beneath his head.

Bolan stepped back from Danny, brought the Beretta around and hit him with a triburst. The guy crumpled at the waist, went to his knees, then fell forward onto his face.

Sam had witnessed the killings in stunned silence, his face turning a pasty white. He started forward, holding out one hand to ward off whatever he thought was coming. Bolan moved in and whipped the Beretta across Sam's face. He stumbled back against the wall and slid down to a sitting position, unconscious.

"I hope they paid you enough," Bolan said.

Smoke hazed the stale air. Brass shell casings rolled across the concrete floor. Bolan took a deep breath, collecting his thoughts, then crossed to pick up his bags. He hung the ordnance bag from his left shoulder and carried the leather satchel in his left hand.

The door opened easily. Bolan was faced with a wide, low-ceilinged cellar. Most of the floor space was filled by cartons and boxes holding electronic items—DVD players, television sets. There was also branded liquor and cigars. He didn't have the time to check it all out. With this kind of merchandise on hand Bolan realized others had to be watching over the cellar. He located the stone steps that led topside and went up fast.

19

Bolan paused at the top of the steps. There was no door, just an opening, and he peered around the edge to see that he was in a large, rundown industrial warehouse. The floor was littered with old machinery, fuel drums and a couple of rusting trucks, sitting on cracked, flat tires. To Bolan's left, high metal doors, pushed open on their slides, showed the exterior. More abandoned machinery and debris. A light breeze stirred the long grass and weeds that grew up through the concrete. Close to the open doors stood a pair of 4x4s. There was nothing derelict about them—they gleamed under the hot sun.

Bolan took a look around the warehouse and spotted two armed men standing close together, enjoying a smoke break. Each gunner carried a slung SMG. Their casual attitude told Bolan they had not heard the shooting from the basement room. It was a lucky break that the Beretta made little noise when fired. The Executioner studied the warehouse and the section outside visible to him, wondering if the two sentries were the only ones around. It was possible there might be others outside. He decided if that was the case he would have to deal with the situation as it arose. He needed to get clear of the warehouse and the restrictions it laid on him. Bolan dropped the money satchel to the floor and lowered his bag to the step and unzipped it. He reached inside and searched through the contents until he found what he was looking for—a couple of stun grenades and his Uzi. He took out his shoulder rig for the Beretta, donned it and holstered the 93-R. The Uzi was loaded with a full clip.

He was aware that in the open space of the warehouse, the stun grenades would lose a percentage of power. They performed best in smaller spaces, where the harsh explosion and the brilliant flash would impact fully. Bolan hoped there would be enough force to at least distract the two sentries and give him time to get within killing range.

Once he had made his decision, Bolan acted on it without further deliberation. He pulled the pins on the canisters and lobbed them both at the pair. The grenades hit the warehouse floor, rolling a few feet closer to the targets even as they spotted them.

One guy gave a startled yell.

The other seemed fascinated by the objects as they slid across the concrete.

The stun grenades detonated within seconds of each other.

Bolan had turned away, covering his ears. He heard the crack of sound and saw the brilliant flash of light as an illumination on the wall. The moment the effects faded, Bolan moved away from the steps, the Uzi cradled in his hands as he loped across the warehouse toward his targets.

The stun grenades had created enough of a disturbance to briefly disorient the two sentries, leaving them with aching ears and altered vision. Even so, they were able to make out Bolan's threatening figure as he closed on them. One groped for his SMG, pulling it into firing position, the muzzle rising.

Bolan already had the Uzi up and ready, tracking his targets. He stroked the trigger, feeling the weapon vibrate as it crackled sharply. The lethal volley of 9 mm slugs cut into the sentries, ravaging flesh and bone. The hot Parabellum rounds impacted with deadly force, spinning the pair in a short twist before they went down, blood staining their clothing and dappling the concrete. The sound of the shots echoed across the open expanse of the warehouse, then faded quickly.

Bolan crossed to the bodies, clearing the dropped weapons away from them.

He was alert to any approaching footsteps, his Uzi trained on the open doorway. Nothing happened. Bolan retrieved his bags. Just as he was about to walk away, he turned and descended the steps into the basement. He took out a couple of prepared explosive packs, set the timers for four minutes and placed them in among the stacked goods. No point in wasting an opportunity to create a little more unrest. If Sam was lucky, he'd make it out.

He made his way outside and picked the closer 4x4. The vehicle was not locked, and the keys were in the ignition. Bolan placed his bags inside, started the engine and eased away from the warehouse. He drove between other empty warehouse buildings until he located the exit ramp and followed it to the deserted service road. Looking around, Bolan could see that the whole of the industrial area was abandoned. At the head of the service road he picked up a sign that indicated the direction back to Cooter's Crossing. He was twelve miles west of the town.

As he drove along the on-ramp for the main highway, Bolan felt the vibration from the explosion at the warehouse. Glancing in his mirror he picked up the telltale rise of smoke.

He used the 4x4's in-car cell phone to call Stony Man Farm. Brognola picked up.

"Good news, or bad?" the big Fed asked.

Bolan brought him up to date, covering his kidnap and the aftermath.

"Dembrow will be starting to worry what's coming next," Brognola said. "Time for a hard strike?"

"Yeah. While he's wavering."

"We got some feedback on the pair you dealt with. A local hit team that called themselves Preacher and Choirboy. It seems they decided on that because, rumor has it, they figured they delivered absolution to their victims. Hell, Striker, killers with a sense of irony. What next?"

"Chris Malloy was part of the snatch team. I think I rattled him when I said we had knowledge of his illegal bank accounts. The guy went a funny color and took off. It might be worth dropping a hint to interested parties. If he's running scared, he might do something stupid."

"Thanks for that. We already initiated a hold on those accounts. Aaron is getting clever with these operations. If Malloy tries to access his money now, he'll get a big shock." Brognola added, "The President is very pleased things are happening. What he really wants to hear about is the total shutdown of the Rojas Cartel."

"Tell him to have a little more patience," Bolan said.

Brognola gave a short chuckle. "You want me to say that to the President of the United States? Striker, I like my job and I want to hang on to it for a while longer."

"You have any feedback from the shoot-out at the packing plant?"

"Feedback? Yeah. Cops found the dead and wounded, and others just standing around wondering why the sky fell in on them. When they were indentified, there were guys from Dembrow's crew and some Rojas Cartel members. DEA was over the moon with the coke they found. It was splashed all over the local news. Nationals got wind of it, too, so if you want I'll put your name forward and you can be this week's instant celebrity."

"I'll pass."

"A certain person who lives at 1600 Pennsylvania Avenue said the news was a complete surprise to him, but considers it a victory in the fight against drug trafficking."

"Good for him," Bolan said dryly.

"Hey, no sulking, big guy."

Bolan gave a soft laugh.

"You might not hear from me for a while," he said. "It's time for a visit to the Dembrow head office. I need to hit while they're still nervous."

"You got everything you need?"

"I need some additional ordnance, and someone who can deliver, then give me a backup ride if I need it. I want to hit hard and fast while they're jumping at shadows."

"Tell me what you need and I'll get it to you quick as I can."

"This needs winding up. The Rojas Cartel has to be leveled, north and south chapters."

"Striker, watch yourself. Nervous or not, these bastards are killers. They don't play around. You invade their home base and they'll fight back."

"I'm expecting that."

20

Bolan sat in the shadows, concealed by dry, dusty scrub oak, scanning the layout of Marshal Dembrow's home base through binoculars. The generously proportioned ranch-style split-level structure was situated about twenty-five miles from Cooter's Crossing, isolated in open country. An amalgam of natural stone and timber blended to form a large house that extended into the surrounding garden, with wide lawns and an even wider patio area. There was an eight-car garage and, beyond the rear of the house itself, a helicopter landing pad. An annex built on the north side of the main house had a cluster of aerials and a rotating radar scanner rising from the roof. The house sat on a parcel of land that stood higher than the surrounding terrain. Bolan imagined that had been a deliberate move during the planning stage.

A number of vehicles were parked at the front of the house, and Bolan saw armed men around the entire perimeter.

It was almost dark. Bolan had reached his current location a couple of hours ago, having parked his newly acquired transport in a dry wash a couple of miles to the south, well away from the approach road. He had suited up with weapons and a large backpack holding additional armament.

The package he had received from Stony Man Farm held some heavy ordnance Bolan had requested in order to back up his standard weapons. He had worked out what he required, doubling up on his request for the follow-up to his hit against Dembrow. The matter of Benito Rojas still had to be resolved, and Bolan wouldn't be waiting around for a second delivery.

His grab bag contained a half-dozen LAWs, incendiary grenades, HE grenades for the M-16/M-203 combo he had asked for, and the Desert Eagle on his hip. His Tanto knife was sheathed on his left side, and his Beretta 93-R was in its customary place in his shoulder leather.

Bolan had met the light aircraft bringing in his ordnance at a civilian airfield a two-hour ride from Cooter's Crossing. He had been waiting when the pilot had rolled the Cessna twin-engine to the standing area.

Bud Casper—a backup pilot originally brought in by Grimaldi for an earlier Executioner mission—owned his own small charter business. Casper had almost died at the end of his first mission with Bolan, but the experience had done nothing to curb his need for action. Casper's aircraft had been totaled at the end of that mission, and Stony Man Farm had replaced it. The tall, lean former Air Force fighter pilot had assisted Bolan on another mission, and had responded positively when asked to fly in some ordnance for Bolan. Jack Grimaldi had been away from the Farm on another mission, so Bolan had no hesitation asking for Casper. He had complete confidence in the man's abilities and his judgment when it came to keeping his mouth shut.

Casper helped Bolan transfer the package to the 4x4.

"Bud, we need to talk," Bolan said.

"Sounds ominous."

In the small café attached to the airfield, Casper had listened as Bolan outlined his upcoming strike against the cartel and the reason for his discretion.

"This is all off the books," Bolan said. "And I mean way off. I'm working this without the knowledge of any agency, or government sanction, because there's no way to get these bastards lawfully. Understand me, Bud, nothing about this has to be linked to the administration."

"You've got my vote, buddy. I know how these drug people work, what they'll do to stay in business. As far as I can see, they don't warrant any consideration. So anything I can do, just ask. And it's between me, you and this coffee mug."

"At this moment you can stick around here and wait for my call. This looks like it's going to be a two-pronged attack—Marshal Dembrow here in Texas, then the main man over in Mexico. You got any aversion to jumping the border?"

Casper raised his coffee mug. "I love Mexico."

BOLAN WATCHED the sun go down, the long shadows merging until the landscape vanished under the night. He saw lights come on around the Dembrow property and settled back to wait. He wanted to stretch the situation, allow Dembrow a little more time to debate what had been happening over the past few days. News of Bolan's escape from the warehouse and the death and destruction he had left behind would have reached Dembrow by this point. Something else for him to think on.

He pulled a water bottle from his pack and took a sip, watching the movement below.

And waited.

21

Dembrow wasn't as vocal as he had been following the diner incident. The recent events had made him reassess his situation. Too much too soon, and it had brought on a mood of self-doubt. Dembrow had looked around him, at his phalanx of armed men, and figured it was going to take more than he had to stop the guy causing his misery.

He couldn't get over how things had progressed, from the diner shoot-out to the interception of the coke delivery with its attendant death toll. And then the man they knew simply as Cooper had faced off with Preacher and Choirboy and walked away leaving them dead. To cap it all, the bastard had taken the drug consignment along with Preacher's classic Lincoln Continental. The embarrassment of the setup in the old meat-packing plant, with Dembrow and Rojas's men shooting at one another, had been made worse when Malloy tracked the guy down, snatched him from his hotel room and took him to the storage warehouse. The slippery son of a bitch had turned the tables, killing Malloy's boys and wiping out Dembrow's warehouse team before blowing the contraband stash to hell. And the stolen drug consignment had been snatched by the DEA.

No one could find Cooper—he seemed to have gone to ground. Planning what? It was the not knowing that unnerved Dembrow. He was used to having his finger on the pulse, knowing every move made in his territory. Cooper had changed all that. He had stirred the pot, pushed everyone to the edge and left them high and dry.

Dembrow had a bad feeling that Cooper was working something that would explode in their faces. The drug lord had pulled in as many of his people to the house as he could and had put extra guards on the grounds. If Cooper wanted a fight to the finish, he would have to come to Dembrow's home ground for it.

Even so, he was nervous. He admitted he'd been drinking too much, but he needed something to settle his mood. The trouble was it didn't seem to be working.

When someone rapped on his study door, Dembrow jerked around, spilling some of the contents from his tumbler onto the carpet.

"Yeah?"

"It's me."

Billy Joe Rankin. The voice was unmistakable.

"What?"

"You got a visitor," Rankin said, pushing open the door.

Chris Malloy followed Rankin into the study. The cop looked worse for wear, his clothing wrinkled and his face drawn. He looked to have aged ten years.

"Jesus, you look fuckin' terrible," Dembrow said, almost relieved to see someone in a worse state then he was. "But after what you did I'm not surprised. You blew our only chance of getting rid of Cooper. Your dumb-ass boys let the guy walk after he had trashed my warehouse. You realize how much that stuff was worth?"

Dembrow spun and hurled his tumbler at the closest wall. It shattered and sprayed glass and whisky across the floor.

"Goddamn it, what were you screwing around with him for? Once you had him at the warehouse all it needed was a bullet in the back of his head. What the hell were you doing?"

"It was a chance to get information out of him. We needed to find out what he had on us. Who sent him," Malloy said.

"No. You should have finished him. Dead he would have

been out of my fucking hair. I told you to get rid of him, not play supercop. Christ, Malloy, you stopped being a cop a long time ago."

"Yeah? If it hadn't been for me, you might not have realized you had a Fed in your organization. You wouldn't have gotten your hands on him if I hadn't passed the information on. I don't give a shit what you think of me as a cop. It wasn't me who let a DEA agent sucker me."

Even Rankin was surprised at Dembrow's speed as he lunged for Malloy. His bunched right fist slammed into the cop's face, tearing at his cheekbone as flesh split. Blood welled from the raw wound. The terrible force behind the blow sent Malloy staggering, his mouth gaping in shock. He crashed against Dembrow's heavy desk, twisting in pain as his left hip took the impact. Dembrow was on him before he could recover. His fists pounded Malloy's face and body, and before Rankin could drag his employer away, Malloy was sagging to his knees, moaning. His face was a mask of bloody flesh. It ran from the wounds, dripping down his shirtfront. He held up a hand in a silent plea for mercy, but Dembrow simply rained more blows on the man, using his feet, delivering crippling blows to Malloy's body.

"Son of a bitch comes into my house and insults me. He blames me for what's been happening. He takes my money and screws up, then blames me."

"Easy, Marshal. Easy," Rankin cautioned. "He's not worth it. The man is finished anyhow. That's why he came out here."

"Say what?"

Dembrow stepped away from Malloy, leaving the shaking, sobbing, bloody figure curled up on the floor.

"When he had Cooper at the warehouse," Rankin said, "the guy told Malloy they had found his bank accounts. The ones where he deposited the money you paid him. Cooper said the money had been frozen. That he couldn't get to it. It was true. When Malloy tried to access his accounts, they had been emptied. He came to see you for help."

Dembrow laughed. "He wants me to help him? He lets Cooper walk, then crawls to me? Don't I have enough to deal with?"

Rankin saw a look in Dembrow's eyes that he hadn't seen in a long time. It made him realize the state of his boss's mind. When the man reached under the back of his jacket, Rankin knew exactly what was going to happen.

"Marshal."

Dembrow ignored him.

He produced a brushed steel pistol, his thumb pushing off the safety, turned the weapon at the back of Malloy's skull and triggered two shots. The 9 mm slugs blew out the front, creating bloody, bone-sharded exit wounds. Malloy jerked forward, slamming against the desk, and slumped loosely, his arms flapping for a time.

The crash of footsteps sounded. The study door flew open and armed figures crowded into the room.

"It's okay," Dembrow said. "Somebody get this mess out of here."

"Hell, Marshal, did that have to happen?" Rankin asked.

"He was on the edge. Ready to give it all up. If he got himself cornered, he would have been telling everything he knew just to save himself. And he knew a lot." Dembrow smiled. "The DEA would have been wetting its pants with the stuff Malloy could have told them. So I made sure that couldn't happen."

Rankin wasn't disturbed by the actual killing. It wasn't the first time he had witnessed violent death. He was more concerned at the way Dembrow was acting. The man showed a tough face and had a commanding presence. Rankin had known him a long time. He understood Dembrow better than most and he was aware of the man's weakness when it came to dealing with stress. In truth, Dembrow was not very good at keeping it together. Killing Malloy was an indication that the overall situation was getting under his skin.

Rankin watched Malloy's bloody corpse as it was carried from the study. He touched Dembrow's arm. "Put the gun away, Marshal. Okay? Let's go relax. Maybe get a sandwich. Some coffee."

The expression on Dembrow's broad face eased, his color

returning to normal. He slid the pistol back under his jacket and followed Rankin out of the room.

"I've got to get things sorted. All this crap with this Lone Ranger running around. And Rojas. Okay, I figured Cooper pointed us at each other over the coke stash. But I still don't trust Rojas. All this goin' on and the bastard hasn't spoken to me once. We're supposed to be partners for Chrissake. I just keep thinking about this missile thing he's trucking in. He could bounce us all the way out of fuckin' Texas with one of those things. We can't ignore the fact, Billy Joe."

As they moved in the direction of the kitchen, Dembrow stopped and stared out of a large window.

"What?" Rankin asked.

"Just a feeling that bastard Cooper is around somewhere. Better tell the boys to be extra sharp tonight."

"Whatever you want, Marshal. Let's go get that coffee, then I'll put the word out."

22

Bolan had noticed the compound standing some way off the main property. It consisted of a few huts and a communal cookhouse. Dembrow would not have tolerated a private community so close to his house, so Bolan thought it housed the domestic staff who catered to the trafficker's needs. The Executioner had studied the grounds before it got too dark. He worked his way around to the compound, taking time to fully observe the inhabitants. He figured there were about ten to fifteen workers. They were all Mexican, with about an equal number of men and women, and several young children. He could hear music playing, coming from one of the huts. He smelled the rich aroma of food wafting from the cookhouse, where three of the women were working. There were no signs of any form of transport around the compound. Dembrow most likely wouldn't want any of his domestic staff wandering far from the house. Bolan suspected that these people were probably illegals, here under sufferance. As long as they remained in Dembrow's employ, he would keep them safe from the authorities. It was an educated guess but Bolan was confident he was right.

He watched as a lone figure wandered across the open compound to perch himself on an upturned wooden pail. The man was elderly, his thick hair starting to gray. He pulled a long, thin cigar from the pocket of his faded denim shirt, lit it and took a slow drag, savoring the aroma.

Bolan eased himself over the crumbling wall and stepped up behind the man. As quiet as he was, Bolan knew he had been sensed as the man's shoulder raised slightly.

"I am a friend. I will not harm you," Bolan said in Spanish, speaking slowly to get the words correct.

"Then show yourself," the man said in clear, accented English.

Bolan walked around the seated man. He was fully armed, so he kept both hands well clear of his body. The old man took in the tall, black-clad figure, missing nothing as he looked over the weapons hanging from Bolan's body. He drew on his cigar. When he finally stared into Bolan's eyes, a gentle smile curved his lips.

"You would not need so many guns if you had come to kill us," he said. "We would not offer any resistance. So I must assume you have come to rid us of the *cucarachas* who live in the big house? The grand house."

"I have work there." Bolan studied the old man, trying to sense any degree of animosity. There was none. "Dembrow gives you shelter. Employs you. If I succeed, you will have no more work."

The old man found that amusing. He gestured at the huts. "He allows us to live here and gives us rations and allows us the privilege of caring for his house and the people who live there. So you think we should be grateful that he knows we cannot leave? Or speak to the *policía?* We came to America as illegals. His men caught us at the border. They brought us here and said as long as we work at the house we were safe. So we have no choice, *señor.* Is it not funny? We crossed into this country to be free. Instead we became slaves for these traffickers. These sellers of poison."

"I don't wish to bring you more bad luck."

The old man shrugged. "If God wishes," he said.

"Tell me. Are any of your people in the house tonight?"

"No. Once our main work was complete Dembrow sent us

back here. He insisted we stay away. Does he know you are coming?"

"Maybe he has a premonition."

"For the past few days he has been acting strangely. I have seen this myself. He has been a nervous man. Tell me, my friend, is this your doing?"

"I may have had something to do with it."

"Then visit them with the wrath of God. They are evil men. They should be treated without pity. In that house I have seen how they force themselves on our women. The young ones especially. Animals would not behave this way to one another."

"Keep your people close tonight. Make sure they do not stray outside the compound. Whatever you see or hear, stay away. Understand?"

"Sí."

Bolan touched the old man on the shoulder, felt his bony hand as it grasped his own.

"Vaya con Dios."

The old man watched as Bolan moved away, back across the wall. He continued to watch even after the tall American merged with the darkness. He looked beyond, to the big house, bathed in the cold glare from the security lights playing on it, and he offered a silent prayer—not for the American—but for the damned souls of the traffickers who were about to be sent to Hell.

23

Bolan eased into position on the ground. He could see the grouped vehicles at the front of the house. The security lights offered him a clear target area. The soldier eased the nylon sling off his back, placed it on the ground beside him and withdrew three of his half-dozen LAWs. He waited until any visible sentries had their backs to him, then raised himself into a kneeling position. Bolan picked up the first LAW and slid out the firing tube, arming the weapon. He laid it across his right shoulder, his cheek snug against the tube, and sighted in on his first target. His fingers pressed down on the firing lever. The M72 launched its missile with a throaty roar. The flash of ignition lit up the darkness as the missile streaked toward the target, arming itself as it flew. Bolan discarded the used launcher and picked up the second LAW while he watched the expensive SUV blow apart as the missile struck, heat flash destroying the interior. The gas tank ignited, exploding with a solid thump, the expended energy lifting the SUV's rear off the ground. The stricken vehicle stood on end for seconds before crashing back to earth. Fire and smoke billowed from the wreck.

The second LAW repeated the actions of the initial hit. This time Bolan went for an almost identical vehicle standing in the center of the parked vehicles. The force from the blast threw this car over on its side, smashing its considerable weight across a sleek Lamborghini Murciélago. The quarter-million-dollar car was crushed by the SUV. The fiery ball of flame completed the destruction of the Italian sports car. When Bolan added the third missile to the conflagration, he saw a Ferrari 575M Maranello and a Porsche GT2 vanish in the expensive flames, chunks of classic bodywork deposited across Dembrow's frontage.

Tucking the three remaining LAWs under his arm, Bolan moved quickly around the perimeter of the grounds, kneeling again as he spotted the rotating radar dish situated on top of the outbuilding attached to the main house. He hit the radar housing with his first missile. The explosion tilted the dish, but it continued to rotate. Bolan unleashed a second missile. The extent of the weapon's destructive abilities was being stretched with a target like this—Bolan made sure his follow-up hit was closer on target. This time the dish canted, then collapsed onto the roof. Bolan used his third missile on the single window, moving dangerously close as he sighted in. He followed the flash trail of the missile as it curved, shattered the window and exploded inside the control room.

The crackle of automatic fire warned the Executioner he had been spotted. He heard the whine and zip of slugs as Dembrow's security crew opened up. For the moment, he still had the advantage of being away from the lights, in darkness—but that might not last. So Bolan moved, staying low, taking himself around the house, away from the burning vehicles and the damaged radar installation.

In the distance he heard shouting. There seemed to be much confusion as the opposition attempted to comprehend what was happening. Bolan's hard strike had caught the Dembrow crew napping and he needed to capitalize on that.

The soldier dropped to one knee, swinging the slung M-16 into position. Bolan pulled an HE grenade from his pouch and loaded it into the M-203 launcher.

The Executioner realized he would have to move in close to take on the Dembrow gunners—and he was more than ready. He needed to engage quickly before they grouped into some form of defensive resistance. The situation was not new to the big American. His blitz maneuver worked well against an unregulated enemy. Dembrow's crew was not composed of trained military personnel. They were basically street thugs, more used to facing unarmed and threatened civilians. On this night they were up against a man steeped in combat, with a determination to win that they would never understand. It did not mean Bolan was going to have an easy time. He never treated his opponents with less than total respect. A casual shot from any weapon could be the one that put Bolan down. The Executioner always faced down every enemy soldier as if they were the best of the best.

Bolan moved to the side of the house away from the burning vehicles, aiming for a shadowed area. He got to within twenty-five feet of the side wall before his approach was spotted and a gunner raced to intercept.

The M-16 spit out a triburst, the 5.56 mm slugs finding their target and dropping the running man in his tracks as they hit the guy's heart. Bolan checked behind, saw he was clear and moved on. He flattened against the wall of the house as a couple more hardmen advanced on his position. He let the pair get close before he leaned out and hit them with twin 3-round bursts. The men went down hard.

Slugs peppered the stone wall a few inches from Bolan's position. He dropped and rolled, staying at ground level, and returned fire. His first shots hit the closest attacker full in the face, toppling the screaming man backward, his blood spattering the face of his unnerved partner. The second guy paused to wipe the sticky blood from his face—it was his last ever mistake. Bolan's 3-round burst stopped him dead.

A window made the Executioner pause in midstride. He turned the rifle in the direction of the glass and fired a burst to shatter it, then triggered the M-203, sending an HE grenade into the house just before he stepped by the window. As the bomb detonated with a hard sound, debris blowing from the frame, Bolan plucked another round from his pouch and loaded it into the launcher.

He dropped to one knee, close to the wall of the house, and laid down tribursts at the figures in front of him, his accurate fire dropping the armed resistance one after another. Return fire was haphazard, the gunners shooting wild at a target they could barely see in the darkness, while Bolan had his targets backlit by the burning vehicles.

The soldier picked up the sound of someone moving behind him. He spun, the M-16 tracking with him, and heard the crackle of automatic fire as slugs chipped into the wall to his left. Bolan felt the sting of a close shot across his upper arm, ignored it and hit the shooter head-on. His own shots were delivered with unerring accuracy. The shooter went down with a moan, his right hip shattered and bloody. A second burst raked the guy's skull, taking away a large chunk of bone and brain matter.

A lull in the resistance prompted Bolan to backtrack. He reached the blown-out window and stepped over the low sill into the room. The HE grenade had laid waste to the interior, splintering furniture and blackening the walls. A hunched figure lay against one wall, flesh riven from bone in a glistening display. The guy still had his rifle clutched in a shriveled hand. Bolan stepped across the floor and peered around the door frame into the passage beyond, checking it out. The corridor seemed to end in a blank wall to his left, the right side taking him deeper into the house.

His move from outside had left the defenders without a target. Before they realized he had changed position, Bolan used the brief calm to his advantage. He ejected the spent magazine from the M-16 and rammed home a fresh one. As he worked the cocking mechanism, Bolan noticed an armed figure straight ahead as the guy stepped into view from the base of a flight of stairs. He shouldered the rifle and dropped the man with a burst to the torso. The guy stumbled and crashed headlong into the wall, leaving a bloody smear on the smooth plaster surface.

A yell of alarm was followed by a gunner leaning over the stair and aiming down at the intruder with a stubby SMG. Bolan dug in his heels and powered forward, dropping and rolling. He heard the harsh rattle of gunfire, the crack of the shots against the tiled floor of the passage. In the seconds he was down, Bolan twisted onto his back, raising the M-16, and raked the stairs with a double triburst. His target arched back, his chest riddled with 5.56 mm slugs. He fell back against the stairs, sliding down to within feet of the base.

Standing again, Bolan tilted the M-16 and fired the M-203, sending the HE round toward the head of the stairs. The blast ripped at the walls and brought down a section of ceiling in a shower of debris and rolling clouds of dust.

Beyond the stairs a door stood ajar. Bolan booted it open and saw a furnished room. From the right side of his combat harness he pulled an AN-M14 TH3 incendiary grenade. Gripping the canister, he pulled the pin, leaned in the open door and dropped the grenade onto the carpeted floor, rolling it away from him. The AN had an extremely short fuse, no more than two seconds. Even as Bolan turned away, the grenade cooked up, releasing 800 grams of thermate that would burn for forty seconds at 2200°C, and was capable of melting through a half-inch homogeneous steel plate. The intense heat generated would turn the room into a raging inferno, consuming anything within range.

Bolan moved across the open hall at the end of the passage. He heard men calling to one another and noted the signs of panic in their voices. He kicked open the double doors in front of him. As the doors swung wide, Bolan saw three gunners turn. But before they had completely faced about, he caught them with repeated tribursts from the M-16. Bodies shuddered, flesh punctured and bones splintered as Bolan dropped the would-be shooters, their blood pooling on the polished wood floor.

Inside the room he used precious seconds to reload the M-203 launcher with an HE round. Before he exited the room he dropped a second incendiary canister, feeling the heat already starting to spread as he cleared the door.

Just beyond Bolan's position, the hall gave way to a generous living area where darting figures scrambled for cover behind furniture. Having easily spotted the men, Bolan triggered the HE grenade and pulled back for cover as the round sizzled into the large room. The crash of the explosion vibrated against the walls, framed pictures dropping from their hooks and smashing on the floor. When Bolan turned back to survey the grenade-blasted living room, he saw a bloodied man stagger upright from the shredded couch he'd been concealed behind. The guy was bloody faced, and his left arm, equally blood streaked, hung loosely at his side. The limb was almost severed at the shoulder, the flesh torn wide and showing bone. Blood pumped from the deep, pulped wound. A triburst from the M-16 dropped the guy to the scorched floor.

Behind Bolan smoke was curling out from the rooms where he had delivered his incendiary bombs. Flames licked out of doorways, rising toward the ceiling and the thick supporting timber beams.

MARSHAL DEMBROW, disbelieving the continuous sounds of destruction, felt the house shudder under the explosions. Overhead the lights flickered; gunfire rattled beyond his study; men were shouting. Whatever Dembrow had been expecting, it didn't match up to the reality of the situation. It felt and sounded as if an army had invaded his home. He crossed the study, yanked open the doors to the gun cabinet and snatched a Franchi SPAS-15 shotgun. The powerful 12-gauge, semiautomatic weapon held a 6-shot magazine. Dembrow picked up a couple more, then headed for the study door. He yanked it open and looked straight into Hell.

The sprawling living area had been destroyed. Furniture and decorations had been reduced to smoking debris. A number of bodies were sprawled across the floor.

He saw Billy Joe Rankin, on his hands and knees, crawling aimlessly across the floor. His adviser had lost part of his face, leaving bloody pits where his eyes had been. Rankin lifted one shredded hand, his fingers missing, as soft sounds came from his bloody, dribbling mouth.

Sickness rose from Dembrow's stomach, and he tore his gaze away from Rankin. His eyes rested on the tall, black-clad figure on the far side of the room, an M-16 cradled against his hip. Dembrow knew who he was looking at—the man who had set off the train of events culminating in this destructive slaughter. There was something in the way the lone man stood there, overseeing the ruination of Dembrow's life and organization, that made him shudder.

"All this because of a fucking federal agent?" Dembrow shouted.

"More than just that," Bolan said. "For *all* the death and suffering you've caused. It stacks up, Dembrow. It stacks up very high, and there's only one way to deal with vermin like you. Extermination."

The scream of pure rage that exploded from Dembrow's throat preempted the raising of the shotgun, his finger curling around the trigger. He felt the weapon jerk, heard the thunder of the shot, then wondered why the blast was directed at the ceiling. His body had already reacted to the slam of the 5.56 mm slugs from Bolan's M-16. The force slammed Dembrow back against the study door frame. He felt the pain, a spreading fire inside his chest, and when he coughed, a surge of blood burst from his lips. Bolan's second burst tore at the man's throat, and the trafficker dropped to his knees. Through the haze of smoke, Dembrow saw the man in black raise the rifle again and watched the smoke trail as he fired the grenade launcher. The grenade curved over Dembrow's head and exploded inside the study. The blast hurled books from shelves and threw the big desk against the wall. Debris blew out the door, shredding the flesh of Dembrow's back.

Bolan took the last of his incendiary grenades and threw it into the big room, where the swell of incandescent heat became a raging torrent of white-hot fury. As he let go of the canister, Bolan turned and moved on, ready to face whatever was left of Dembrow's crew.

Slumped against the door frame, struggling for his final breath, Dembrow felt the hungry maw of the terrible fire as it expanded to engulf the room. The intense heat blistered his flesh, sloughing it from his bones, igniting his hair and searing his eyeballs. The last image he had was of Rankin, frozen in a motionless pose, burning up in front of him. His adviser's mouth was wide in a silent scream, but no sound came out, only white and brilliant flame.

24

Bolan met little resistance as he exited the house. The main doors had been opened wide, and the draft that was pulled into the house helped fan the increasing flames at his back. Smoke billowed from windows broken by the intense heat. Only two armed figures moved to confront him, but Bolan was in no kind of mood to play games. His M-16 crackled in the half-light, the 5.56 mm slugs punching into yielding flesh and driving the pair to the ground.

Searching for any remaining gunners Bolan stalked the grounds, circling until he was at the rear, facing the parked helicopter. He thumbed an HE grenade into the launcher and fired on the chopper. The bomb hit at the rear of the cabin, the blast tearing the alloy fuselage to shreds. Bolan had cleared the site when the ruptured tank blew, scattering blazing fuel in every direction.

The Executioner made his slow return to where he had hidden his ride. He changed clothes and stowed his weapons. The bullet crease on his arm turned out to be nothing more than that. His blacksuit had taken the worst, leaving a slit in the material, but Bolan's flesh had barely been marked. Thinking back, he considered himself lucky. Once again, his walk through the hellgrounds had left him unscathed, the enemy brought to its knees. Bolan put his quick success down to Dembrow's crew having been caught unaware, their responses too slow. It reinforced his belief that the trafficker's team was unschooled in real combat. They threatened and bullied, used physical violence on ordinary people who had little recourse. An attack by a combat-experienced soldier showed them to be no more than swaggering novices who carried guns but were not trained in outright defense and resistance tactics.

The wound reminded Bolan that he was still mortal. He never allowed himself to become complacent. He carried his war directly to his enemies, took his knocks when it was his turn and never complained about it. The day he doubted himself would be the day he started to lose. The Executioner had no intention of allowing that day to come. If self-doubt ever did weaken his resolve, he would voluntarily step down. He might never have expressed that viewpoint to anyone, but he understood it himself, and that was enough for the time being.

As he climbed back in the 4x4 and started the engine, he took a final look back. Dembrow's house was fully ablaze. The flames reached high into the night sky, throwing an orange glow that would have been seen for miles—if there had been anyone in the area to see them.

Bolan called Stony Man Farm on the 4x4's cell phone. When Brognola came on, the soldier gave him a quick update.

"One down," the big Fed said. "I expect I'll be hearing about it on the news. How much do you want to wager this will be reported as another drug gang fallout?"

"Hal, there was some collateral fallout to this. I want you to make it right. Even if you have to bend the President's arm."

"Hell, Striker, that's the second time you've suggested I harass the Man. Trying to make me lose my pension?"

The big Fed sighed. "Go on."

The Executioner filled him in about the domestic staff, and the fact that with Dembrow out of the picture they were defenseless and had no means to provide for themselves—and it had been Bolan who had made that happen.

"I'm working for you and the President, so that ties us all in to this. Those people need help, Hal. Dembrow held them against their will, threatened them and treated them badly. Do the right thing."

"Times are, Striker, you would make a damn good lawyer. You plead a good defense. Okay, I'll look into it."

"Thanks," Bolan said. "So anything I need to know?"

"Yeah. Give your buddy Seminov a call. He says he has something that will make you smile."

"GOOD TO HEAR your voice, *tovarich*," Valentine Seminov boomed over the speaker. "It is true what I hear—that you have Vash Bondarchik on your current agenda? Tell me this is truly so."

Bolan sketched the Russian arms dealer's connection to his mission. Seminov listened in silence, then exhaled a heavy sigh.

"I want that bastard so bad it hurts." Seminov added a quick string of words in Russian that Bolan had difficulty understanding, but he recognized the passion in Seminov's outburst.

"Hey, Valentine, I get the message."

"Yes. I get carried away when I think about Bondarchik. I have been after him for too long."

"So let's see what we can do about him. The world could do with one less arms dealer."

"The word is that Bondarchik has negotiated to supply Spyker ex-military portable missile units to this Mexican, Rojas. Yes?"

"Rojas is flexing his muscle. He runs a powerful cartel supplying illegal drugs to the U.S. I just shut down his American partner, so Rojas is not going to be a happy man. The guy is a lowlife, and he's ruthless. If he got his hands on these missiles, I have no doubt he'd use them on U.S. targets."

"And your DEA? They cannot stop him?"

"Same old, same old. Rojas resides on Mexican soil. Technically he's their problem, but the man has protection on all levels. No one will acknowledge he's a problem. Hell, Valentine, we know how it works. Bondarchik has his friends in government and the police. That, plus his expensive lawyers, and he can fend off any threat."

"I understand only too well. This is why I am unable to bring Bondarchik to his knees. Every time I get at arm's length I am ordered to back off."

"Our DEA is restricted by law, Valentine. I'm not. If Bondarchik is supplying weapons to Rojas, then he's on the hit list, too."

Seminov didn't hesitate. "Then I am with you, *tovarich*. Whatever it takes."

"Tell me what you have."

"I have been doing a little private snooping, using non-OCD sources. When you have been in this business as long as I have, well, it pays to have informants out of the spotlight. You understand?"

"Yeah," Bolan replied.

"This friend has means to find out information. I asked him to check into Bondarchik's business. He was reluctant because he has respect for Bondarchik's methods. If he was discovered asking too many questions, his death would not be pleasant."

"I understand."

"But this friend owes me favors. Big favors. So I leaned on him and he went away. It took him only a day before he brought me useful data. I didn't ask him how he got it. I paid him for his troubles, and he told me what he had learned. I don't want to bore you with all the details, *tovarich*. Only what I believe might be really what you are looking for."

"I'm listening, Valentine."

"Bondarchik owns an oil transportation company based in Venezuela. It is situated on the Maracaibo Basin. As companies go, this one is only medium sized. No more than six smaller oil tankers. When we accessed the shipping manifests, something struck me as odd. Over the past eight months, Bondarchik's tankers have made deliveries to a number of destinations where we know he has customers for his weapons sales."

"You think he's using his oil tankers to deliver his arms?"

"It crossed my mind. It became even more definite when I saw where a current cargo is being delivered—"

"Mexico. Dammit, Valentine, that could be the missile launchers for Rojas."

"We ran a search and found that the tanker is indeed bound for a port in the Gulf of Mexico. A small oil refinery on the eastern coast of the country near a town named Agua Verde."

"Too much going on here for it to be a coincidence."

"Pah, I do not believe in such things, *tovarich*."

"Make that two of us," Bolan said. "When is that tanker supposed to dock?"

"It should be there in a few days."

"My next destination, then."

"I wish I was going to be there with you, *tovarich*."

"Valentine, you've pushed me in the right direction. I owe you on this."

Seminov laughed. "Don't worry, I'll collect one day. If I find out any more I will call. You take care. *Dasvidaniya*."

25

"Is there a problem?" Bondarchik asked.

"Rojas is impatient. He wants his cargo."

Bondarchik heard his knuckles creak as he gripped hard on the phone. "He knows I can't move it any faster. The ship is not a damned speedboat. It will arrive on time. On the agreed date." He allowed a heartbeat's pause. "Tell me everything, Tibor. What is wrong?" the arms dealer asked.

"Rojas is under pressure here. He's having a troubling time. There is bad feeling between him and Dembrow. Rojas figures Dembrow is losing it. He let a DEA undercover agent into his organization and didn't find out until the guy had wormed his way well into the group. The agent's dead, but soon after that there was a face-off between a bunch of Rojas's people and some of Dembrow's. It ended in a shooting match, with dead on both sides. This created tension in both camps."

"Perhaps this as an opportunity for us to increase business," Bondarchik suggested.

Tibor Danko laughed. "I was thinking the same thing," he said. "See an opening and go for it."

After the call ended, Bondarchik leaned back in his comfortable armchair and considered the possibilities. Two strong factions on the brink of hostilities? If he could profit from that, all to the good.

Bondarchik, at thirty-six years old, was a proved dealer in the arms-dealing business—an extremely successful dealer. His customer base was global. He sold to anyone, anywhere, supplying whatever they wanted as long as their money was on the table. Bondarchik had clients in Asia, the Middle East and Central America. His weapons were in Africa, and any of a dozen other worldwide hotspots. The new century had not heralded in a new era of peace. If anything, violent conflict was on the increase, and while that continued, Bondarchik would stay in business. His motto was that as long as a client had the cash, he could buy what he wanted. Bondarchik didn't care how the weapons were used, or on whom. He believed that if people got shot they most likely deserved it.

He pushed up from the chair and crossed the expensively furnished room, selected a cigarette from the case on his desk and lit up. Tall and in top physical shape, Bondarchik was a good-looking man. He kept himself that way by regular bouts in the well-equipped gym installed in his expansive house. It contained the best money could buy. That was his attitude toward everything he possessed. What point was there in making vast amounts of money if he didn't use it to maintain his lifestyle? Good living, clothes, cars. Bondarchik enjoyed the rewards of his business. He surrounded himself with luxury, including the women he courted, and he maintained the same attitude toward the people he employed. He paid them well, looked after them, and in return they gave him dedication and loyalty.

Beyond the soundproof glass wall of the room, a wide patio area fronted a generous swimming pool, the water reflecting the sunlight. Two of his men, armed, kept watch over the area, and also over the trio of nubile young women who frolicked on the patio and in the pool. Bondarchik didn't begrudge the guards their pleasure. He would have worried if they had not been attracted by healthy, half naked young women unashamedly displaying their bodies.

Despite the charms of the girls, Bondarchik found he was unable to dismiss what Danko had told him about the situation in Texas and Mexico. He crossed to his desk and hit the intercom button, putting out a call for Danko, who was in his own office on the far side of the house.

"Come into my office," he said, when the man came on the line. "We need to talk more about this."

Tibor Danko, a medium height man with the physique of a bodybuilder, always dressed in a well-cut suit, with a shirt and tie. His shaved head added to the air of menace he displayed, yet behind that he possessed a sharp brain and everyone in the Bondarchik organization regarded him with the utmost respect. He had worked with Bondarchik for almost ten years. His past remained a secret between himself and his employer. Rumors went around that he had once been in the army and had the skills of a special forces operative, and no one thought of challenging the rumors. Fact, not rumor, was Danko's skill with any weapon he might have in his hand.

"Rojas is getting nervous," Danko said. "He is talking about canceling the order. A lot is happening, and he can't seem to get a grip on it. I tried to calm him down. To make him see sense."

"Cancel the order?" Bondarchik's anger spilled over. "No. He can't do that. Doesn't he realize the effort that has gone into shipping that cargo? How much I have invested? This isn't a case of AK-47s. The Spyker missile system is a complex item. No. I will not accept this." He raised his hands. "The shipment is on schedule. Why would he want to cancel?"

"As I explained, there seems to be some local problem with his American counterpart. Some kind of fallout. I could sense Rojas is nervous. He needs to assert his superiority, so Rojas is demanding we hurry the delivery, or he might cancel."

"What does he expect? That we order the tanker's crew to get out the oars and row faster?"

"I agree," Danko said. "There's no way we can speed delivery. I just thought you should know in case the matter comes up again when you meet with Rojas."

"He is bluffing, making waves when there is no need. If he cancels, he will harm no one but himself. He admits he needs the missiles, so what game is he playing?"

Danko nodded. "He needs talking to. Pay him this visit and

talk him around." He paused. "But first we have a local problem of our own that has come up."

"Let me guess, Tibor. Is it to do with our old friend Seminov?"

"You know, I believe you enjoy spoiling my announcements," Danko said.

"What is our OCD friend up to now?"

"A couple of days ago he hassled a couple of our people in Moscow. Dragged them in for questioning. Again."

"But our lawyers stepped in and had them released?"

"Of course. Seminov got nothing. Vash, that damn cop is becoming a nuisance. Why don't we deal with him?"

"If we kill Seminov, they will simply appoint someone else. At least we know Seminov and understand his ways. He's a good policeman. Very thorough. Experienced."

"That is what worries me, Vash. One day he might get the break he's been looking for. Then what?"

"Tibor, the other reason we don't do anything about Seminov is simple. Kill a cop and the whole damn force will start a hunt that will drag us all in. Every case he's ever worked will be reopened. Every major and minor criminal will be hauled in for questioning. And somewhere along the line someone might start talking. It's less of a risk to leave Seminov alone. We can handle anything he throws our way." Bondarchik laughed. "It's why we have that bunch of overpriced lawyers on standby. For just those occasions."

Bondarchik crossed to the panoramic window and stood looking out beyond the perimeter of his property to the shimmering water of the Black Sea. The weather was superb. He enjoyed the view, as always, but he understood that there was business to attend to. What a pity, he decided. But it would all be here when he returned.

"The plane is ready anytime you want to go," Danko said, anticipating Bondarchik's next question.

"A trip to sunny Mexico?"

"Client satisfaction," Danko said, grinning.

"Is Litvenko on standby?"

"Looking forward to the trip."

"Then I have no choice," Bondarchik stated.

"Litvenko has all his data with him. He will meet you at the airstrip."

"Then I can go and not worry?"

"Vash, everything is in order. Go. Perhaps this trip will be good for you. A chance to relax. Yes?"

Bondarchik smiled. "You are like a mother, Tibor."

"Go, just go. I will look after things here."

THE BOEING BUSINESS Jet, the BBJ2, painted in cream and deep blue, was the pride of Bondarchik's fleet. He had purchased it two years previously and on top of the cost, he had the aircraft customized. Extra fuel tanks had been installed to extend its flying distance, and the interior, though already well appointed, had been adapted to Bondarchik's own design sense. Its communication system and onboard computer installation had been updated. The facilities allowed Bondarchik to conduct his business dealings as if he were still at his home base. The Boeing's seating and interior was fitted with deep pile carpeting and plush, cream colored, soft leather executive seats. The passenger section could accommodate up to ten people on single seats and curving couches. There were also four private cabins with king-size beds and a fully equipped entertainment lounge. Food from the onboard kitchen could provide top-class meals. Bondarchik also had his own state-of-the-art office suite. There were two more offices available, and once they were in the air, Karl Litvenko disappeared into one of them to review his manuals and computer data.

Litvenko was Bondarchik's technical adviser. He was accompanying his employer to advise Benito Rojas's people on the operation of the missile system.

From his own office Bondarchik made contact with Rojas to let him know they were en route. The Mexican still hinted he was far from satisfied, but Bondarchik pointed out that regardless of the situation it was necessary for their meeting to take place. Bondarchik sensed something else behind Rojas's minor quibbles over slow delivery of the ordnance. Tapping into the recessed keyboard on the desk, Bondarchik linked up with Danko. The man's image appeared on the flat-screen monitor.

"I expected you to be watching the in-flight movie, Vash. Don't tell me you are still working."

"Dollars do not make themselves, Tibor."

"Dull but true."

"I spoke to Rojas. The man is still grumbling. I have a feeling he is keeping something from me. Here is something you can do. Check to see if you can find out what is making that Mexican peasant such a pain in the ass, then get back to me."

The Boeing took Bondarchik and Litvenko from the Black Sea to a privately owned airstrip in Libya, a few miles from Tripoli. The airfield was owned by a powerful figure in the oil business, a man who had close ties with Bondarchik. The Russian had acquired an interest in the conglomerate running the group of companies, and through discreet fund managing Bondarchik had sunk millions of dollars into the group. Unlike many in the arms business, Bondarchik liked to see his money working for him.

The Boeing touched down and remained on Libyan soil only for as long as it took to top up the fuel tanks. Cleared for takeoff, the pilot eased the jet into the air, then tapped in the coordinates that would take the aircraft over North African airspace and on across the Atlantic, the Gulf of Mexico and eventually touchdown on Rojas's airstrip. The coordinates were locked into the autopilot. The Boeing made flight adjustments until it was on the correct course, then settled smoothly.

Bondarchik checked in with Karl Litvenko. The man was immersed in his manuals. He merely raised a hand at Bondarchik's inquiry and asked for fresh coffee and vodka. Bondarchik passed the request to the cabin staff and resumed his own seat. He settled in the plush leather and tilted the backrest to a low angle. Farther along the cabin his two bodyguards were also relaxing, enjoying the rare time when even their job of looking after Bondarchik was made easy.

They would arrive in Agua Verde early evening. Bondarchik

would be fully rested, and he would refrain from any business talk until the following morning. Bondarchik knew how to conduct his affairs. There was little point being as successful and wealthy as he was if he was unable to enjoy the rewards. The Russian watched the young flight attendant as she walked down the cabin to deliver drinks to his bodyguards. Watching her, he became aware of restless urges stirring. Business had dominated his life 24/7 over the past few weeks, and he had found little time to take out for personal pleasures. He called the woman to his side and ordered a drink, suggesting she bring it to his personal cabin. The flight attendant, a very attractive twenty-year-old, smiled in complete understanding. Bondarchik watched the supple swing of her hips as she made her way to the galley to prepare his drink. He pushed to his feet and made his way to the cabin where he sat on the edge of the bed and waited.

Luckily he didn't have to wait all that long.

"I WAS BUSY," Bondarchik said to Danko over the video link.

"Of course," Danko said. "If I have it right, Dina was on cabin duty this flight. Yes?"

Bondarchik couldn't miss the glint in Danko's eyes. "Very funny. So what was this urgent message you have for me?"

"Rojas's concerns seem to have not been so fanciful. Marshal Dembrow, the majority of his crew and his Texas house are all gone. There was some kind of attack. Dembrow and his men suffered severe casualties. The house was hit, then burned to the ground. By the time the authorities arrived, all they could do was round up the survivors. According to my source, there were bodies spread around the property. Cars and even Dembrow's helicopter had been destroyed," Danko said.

"Who is responsible? The American DEA? Police?"

"No one seems to be accepting responsibility. It is very odd."

"I don't know, Tibor. But this explains why Rojas is becoming so concerned. If there is some threat to his organization, he will want the security of the missile system. He will expect it to save him. And that is exactly what I will tell him. I do not want to walk away from him without the rest of our money in my hand."

"You are a true capitalist," Danko said, grinning widely.

"But of course. It is the one real lesson I have taken from our American friends." Bondarchik leaned closer to the screen. "Do what you can to find out who is behind these attacks, which American agency is involved. We need to know for our own satisfaction. If you know an enemy, you have an advantage."

"Are you landing soon?"

"We are coming in now. I will talk to you later, Tibor."

Danko nodded. "Vash, do not forget to tip the flight attendant."

"But of course."

THE BOEING ROLLED to a stop on the concrete apron. As the engines whined to silence, the door was opened and a mobile ramp was pushed into position. Bondarchik, accompanied by Litvenko and the armed bodyguards, stepped out and walked to the bottom of the steps.

Bondarchik felt the heat immediately. It wrapped itself around him like a warm blanket. There was a long Mercedes limo waiting. The Russian crossed to it and climbed inside, sighing with relief as the chill of the air conditioning hit. He sank into the seat. Litvenko sat beside him, the two burly bodyguards in the rear facing seats. The limo pulled away after luggage was deposited in the trunk.

A young, lean Mexican sat next to the driver. He turned now to greet them.

"Welcome to Mexico, Mr. Bondarchik. I will be looking after you for the present. I am Tomas Trujillo."

26

Chico Morales glanced from the thick wads of U.S. dollars on his desk, to the tall, dark-haired American, then back to the money. He could gauge by the thickness of the bills there was a great deal of money sitting in front of him. Even though an electric fan was whirring close by, sending cool air over him, Morales felt a sheen of perspiration break out on his face. He unconsciously reached up to scrub at his unshaved jaw.

"Tell me again what I have to do, *señor. Por favor.* So there can be no misunderstanding."

"I have private business in Agua Verde. I need a place to park my aircraft. One of your hangars would be ideal."

"And what else?"

"The plane needs to be refueled and kept out of sight. I was told Chico Morales would be able to help, that he is an honest man."

Morales leaned back in his creaking, scuffed swivel chair. He might not have been obese, but he was a big man, his clothing rumpled and stained.

"Who told you these truths about me?"

"A man from Langley who rates you highly."

BOLAN'S INFORMATION had come from Brognola, via a CIA contact the big Fed had known for some years. His agency connection was one of those few outsiders Brognola kept tucked away for special occasions. As far as the CIA man was concerned, Brognola was working out of his Justice Department office and knew nothing about the big Fed's Stony Man Farm connection. Brognola and the CIA man did each other favors from time to time that offered benefits to either man. It was a satisfactory arrangement that worked well.

Brognola had simply asked for a safe contact in the Mexican location, hinting he had something in the pipeline that might have a beneficial result. Once his contact realized the significance of the area, he offered Morales as a local asset.

"Just don't get him compromised."

"All I need is for him to offer a little storage space for a while. No direct involvement."

"Morales is solid, Hal. He has a mercenary streak a mile wide, but he's always done good by us."

"That's all I need, Tom. Put this one on my tab."

"Don't think I won't, buddy."

BUD CASPER HAD FLOWN Bolan to a safe landing on the airstrip carved out of the vegetation, about a mile in from the Gulf coast. Taxiing the twin-engine Cessna to a stop outside the line of hangars, Casper had braked short of the flat-topped building that served as control tower and office. While Casper stayed with the aircraft, Bolan had eased himself from the passenger seat and crossed to the building. He knocked on the door and waited until he was told to enter.

The office smelled of old cigars and stale coffee. There was a busy desk covered with files, shelves overflowing with documents, and the walls were dotted with outdated calendars and pinups.

Lounging in a large, worn leather executive chair was a Mexican in his early forties. His thick black hair was due for a trim and his clothes looked as if they served as his pajamas. He watched as Bolan stepped inside. Despite his outward appearance, Chico Morales had the look of a man with sharp instincts and an equally keen brain.

After the introductions, Morales asked Bolan to take a seat, watching the big American intently. When Bolan produced the wads of cash and offered his proposal Morales became seriously interested.

"This man from Langley has a name?"

"He said to tell you Lightfoot."

Morales nodded. "And what do I call you, *señor?*"

"Cooper."

"May I speak honestly?"

"Yes."

"This is not truly tourist country. You understand?"

"I'm not a tourist and I haven't come to lie on a beach. This is Benito Rojas territory. Not a man who welcomes interference."

Morales smiled. "So you have not come to Agua Verde to wish him well. Or to fish in the bay?"

Bolan shrugged.

"Others have tried to negotiate with Rojas. But he is not a man who indulges others."

"I understand that," Bolan said. "Do we have a deal?"

Morales picked up the money. "*Sí.* We have a deal. You can put your aircraft in hangar three."

"How far to Agua Verde?"

"Two, maybe three miles north from here. On the coast. And before you ask, the Rojas place is another twenty miles up the coast." Morales left his chair and led the Executioner to a large map of the area pinned to the wall. "Agua Verde. Here, within this bay. Rojas has his place overlooking the sea on the eastern edge of the bay."

Bolan ran a finger along the map to a spot between Agua Verde and the Rojas property. A docking facility called Puerto Verde.

"This is where Rojas has his oil terminal?"

Morales nodded. "*Sí.* This is how Rojas appears to be *legítimo.* He runs the dock and the oil distribution here. Most of the laborers are local men—honest men who need the work."

"You don't sound convinced."

"Nothing that hombre has his hands on could be truly honest. There is another side to the business I am sure."

"Thanks for your help, Chico."

Morales smiled. "Thank you, *mi amigo.* Is there anything else you need?"

"A ride to town and the name of someone who can hire me a boat."

"That is easy. I have a spare automobile you can use. Not new, but very reliable. You are most welcome to borrow it. I know who you can hire a boat from. But what are you going to do?"

"I've reconsidered. A little fishing trip will relax me for a while."

"Of course. Hiring a boat is a good way to explore and see the sights."

MORALES HAD SPOKEN the truth about the car. The ride was certainly not new—it was a nondescript American Dodge, easily fifty years old. Age notwithstanding, the vintage engine still had plenty of punch beneath the hood, and Bolan didn't miss seeing that the tires were fairly new, with plenty of deep tread. When he hit the road outside the strip, he found the brakes worked well and the springy ride could have been worse. With his bags in the spacious trunk and Casper at his side, Bolan wheeled the big Dodge toward Agua Verde, keeping his foot light on the gas pedal. He had realized quickly there was power in the engine, and the last thing he wanted was to be pulled over by a Mexican cop for speeding.

27

The dockside was quiet. No one paid a great deal of attention as Bolan parked the Dodge. He and Casper climbed out of the vehicle and stood at the edge of the dock, looking out across the calm waters of the Agua Verde bay. Local boats were drifting back and forth, and Bolan noted there were a few moored along the wooden jetty close by.

"That's the place," Casper said.

He indicated a faded sign hanging loosely to the white frontage of a store displaying marine tackle.

"Stay close, Bud," Bolan said.

He crossed the quay and stepped out of the hot sun into the cool interior. The store was crowded with gear. Bolan sensed movement ahead of him and saw a Mexican wearing a loud shirt over creased blue jeans. The man leaned on the scarred counter.

"I was told you speak English," Bolan said. "My Spanish is a bit rough."

"Do not concern yourself, *señor*. If you have come to do business then we all speak the same language."

"Chico Morales told me you are the man to see about hiring a boat and equipment to fish."

"*Sí*, I can do that. It could be expensive."

"That is not a worry," Bolan said. "My friend and I want to enjoy our free time. You have what I need?"

"Look around, *señor,* and pick what you want."

"I need a good boat, with plenty of fuel."

The man nodded and called for his assistant. He gave orders and the assistant left. He watched as Bolan moved around the store, selecting items he wanted. When the big American returned to the counter and set down his selection, the Mexican's face was covered in a generous smile. He quickly calculated the cost, adding the rental for the boat and fuel. The final figure was high. Bolan spent a few minutes haggling over the price and got a few hundred dollars knocked off. He wasn't going to pay without making a deal. An American paying without worrying over the price might arouse curiosity and draw attention to Bolan and Casper, which was not what the Executioner wanted. A satisfactory price was agreed, and Bolan handed over the cash—more from the satchel of money he had appropriated from the trunk of the Lincoln Continental. It was a small victory making the drug traffickers pay in part for their own downfall.

The boat was ready an hour later. Bolan and Casper boarded along with their equipment for the fishing trip, Bolan's bag containing his ordnance, and a box of provisions purchased from a nearby store. Casper then started the engine and, after Bolan had loosened the lines, he eased the boat away from the jetty and steered it across the bay.

"STRIKER, YOU'VE GOT enough ordnance in there to head up the next Mexican Revolution," Casper said.

"Damned well better not get to that."

Bolan had his weapons spread across the boat's cabin. He was aware of the battle ahead, the numbers up against him. By this time Rojas would have heard what happened to his partner across the border. Bolan figured Rojas to be the smarter of the two. He would assume the responsibility of his position and act accordingly, which meant he would be ready for Bolan. Against the Executioner's favor was the lack of knowledge over how many he might be facing. In his favor was his skill at close-quarters combat, and a willingness to move with the tide and adapt. Sheer numbers, unless thoroughly disciplined and highly trained to fight, didn't guarantee success.

"That offer still stands," Casper said. "And you know I'm no beginner."

"Hell, Bud, you proved that a couple of times. Let's stick with what we already agreed. You go with me as far as the drop-off point, then wait to haul me out. I've got a feeling when I quit it's going to have to be fast."

Casper nodded. "Okay. I'm your man."

The pilot stepped back and watched as Bolan quietly set out his weaponry. He had to admire the way the man went about his business. No rush. The steady, deliberate actions of a man at one with his mission.

Clad in his blacksuit and combat boots, Bolan outfitted himself for the coming assault. His weapons selection was more or less identical to the one for the earlier strike with the addition of a satchel holding a number of six-inch-by-four-inch metal devices. They drew Casper's attention and Bolan handed him one.

"Solid."

Bolan nodded. "Metallic explosive mine," he explained. "Clamp it to the target and activate with the button on the side. It has an integrated timer that runs for ten minutes, then detonates the explosive compound inside. Neat and lethal."

The mines had been worked up and built by the Stony Man Farm resident armorer, John "Cowboy" Kissinger. The man was no slouch when it came to devising deadly weapons for the SOG warriors. The punch delivered by the devices would be enough to lift a 4x4 off the ground even as it was being shredded.

"Striker, you have some dangerous friends."

Bolan smiled at that. Casper didn't know the half of it.

"You want to go start the engine and get us out of here?"

Casper left the cabin and went up on deck. He fired up the powerful boat engine again and left it slowly turning as he went and pulled up the small anchor that had held them while Bolan checked his gear. Back in the wheelhouse Casper increased the power and took the boat forward.

Out of sight below, Bolan placed his ordnance in a long seal-able bag and placed it on one of the side benches. He pulled a loose sweatshirt and a pair of canvas trousers over his blacksuit so he could show himself on deck. Standing next to Casper, studying an area chart spread across the navigation table, Bolan traced their route across the bay. It would take a couple of hours to work their way around to the coastal inlet where Rojas had his estate.

The day was hot and clear. Only a few shreds remained of the early mist that had hung over the surface of the water. They passed a few other boats as they cruised toward their destination.

"Don't you think Rojas is going to be watching every access point to his property?" Casper asked.

"I didn't say it was going to be easy," Bolan said.

BY MIDDAY they had anchored a distance offshore. Casper broke out the gear, and they settled down to some serious fishing. They were not the only boat in the area. Others had anchored, and a number of enthusiasts were trying their luck. Casper had fished before, and he landed a couple of specimens in the first hour.

"You think they're watching?" he asked.

"Maybe," Bolan said. "But they can't suspect every boat that stops in Agua Verde bay."

Bolan took his binoculars and stood in the cover of the wheel-house, scanning the coast in and around the bay. He located the oil terminal. A couple of long jetties stretched out from the main dock, where cranes and container facilities dominated the scene. Behind them there were warehouses and an office block. Swinging the glasses back, Bolan studied the private jetty to one side of the Rojas property. A number of high-power speedboats were tied up to the wooden dock, and twenty feet back from it was a long, low modern building, and on the far side an open area with a smooth, grassed area that curved its way to the Rojas house.

Like the former Dembrow residence, it was large and opulent. Bolan's discreet scan revealed that Rojas had a number of armed guards patrolling the grounds.

"Find what you want?" Casper asked, as Bolan emerged from the wheelhouse, carrying a couple of bottles of chilled beer from the cooler.

"Answered some questions," Bolan said.

He leaned against the rail, his back to the shore, and watched the other boats gently riding the waves. If he had been that way inclined, Bolan could have harbored a little envy for the men in those boats. They were there simply to enjoy the weather and the fishing. When the day was over, they would turn around and return to Agua Verde. Most likely they would end up in a cantina swapping fishing stories.

There would not be any of that for the Executioner. The closest Bolan would get to fishing would be his association with Rojas. The man was a human shark, a predator striking at the heart of civilized man. Rojas fed off the weak, preying on those dependent on the drugs he supplied.

Bolan didn't look too deeply into the craving for drugs as much as the realization of what the stuff was doing to society—it ruined lives, broke up families and encouraged crime in all its forms. And those who were caught in the trap, found themselves hooked on the treadmill, unable to break free. It was an ever-increasing desperation for drugs that made the addicts come back for more, and men like Rojas were always there to feed that need. His moral code had become lost in the dark twist of his soul. Rojas didn't consider the effects of his trade. He only cared about staying top dog and hauling in the flood of money coming his way.

Bolan's work would start with the onset of darkness. He had come to Agua Verde to shut down the Rojas Cartel. The Executioner had started the ball rolling back in Cooter's Crossing, the finale coming about with the destruction of Dembrow's crew and the razing of his house. He had similar work ahead of him.

This time around the target was Rojas and everyone associated with him.

A couple of the fishing boats remained in the area, showing lights against the dark, the exuberant calls of their crews floating across the water as they bragged about the size of their catches. Bolan signaled to Casper. The boat's engine coughed into life. They came about and slid through the quiet water until they rounded the promontory that briefly blocked them from the Rojas property.

Bolan was ready, his face and hands darkened with water-proof combat cosmetics, and a waterproof rubber suit over his blacksuit. He had checked his satellite radio communicator with Casper before he enclosed it under the rubber suit, along with his fully charged cell phone nestled in a blacksuit pocket.

Slipping over the side, Bolan reached up and took the heavy sealed bag that held his weapons as Casper handed it down. He hooked the strap over one arm and let the bag settle in the water. There were a couple of buoyancy pouches built into the bag that kept it floating just below the surface.

"You watch your back, Striker," Casper said. "Make your call and I'll come for you."

Bolan nodded and pushed off from the side of the boat, heading for the rocky shore, the darkness swallowing him quickly.

28

Earlier, as he swam toward the shoreline, Bolan had heard the whine of a jet aircraft overhead. Glancing up, he spotted the lights of a plane coming in to land. It swept overhead, already low, then angled in across what would be Rojas ground space. Bolan recalled mention of a landing strip in the files, but he hadn't realized just how large it might be. When the sound of the jet faded, the soldier turned his attention back to his swimming.

The full moon allowed Bolan enough light to see his way ashore. He had been in the water for three-quarters of an hour, making his way to the rocky shoreline just to the south of the Rojas estate perimeter. He emerged from the warm Gulf water, easing his weapons bag with him, and worked his way into the jumble of rocks.

He worked his way out of the rubber suit, rolled it into a bundle and stuffed it into a gap in the rocks. Then he opened his weapons bag and armed himself with the Beretta and Desert Eagle after checking each weapon. The combat webbing went on next, the pouches already loaded with extra magazines for his complement of weapons, plus incendiary canisters. Bolan slid the Cold Steel Tanto combat knife into place. He slung the satchel holding the magnetic mines across his back, feeling their solid weight, and he hung the Uzi around his neck. The Executioner decided against taking the M-16 this time. With four LAWs he figured he was carrying the maximum—he didn't want to over-burden himself. He could handle a heavy load, but even he had his limits and slowing himself too much was asking for trouble. So he zipped up the rubber bag and concealed it beneath a shallow overhang, covering it with sand and pebbles.

The Executioner climbed the rocky gradient, staying close to the surface until he reached the top. He peered over the lip of the slope. A rough patch of ground stretched into the distance, three hundred yards of exposed terrain that broke where it reached the stone wall marking the border of Rojas land. The solid wall stood about three feet high, not actually intended as a barrier but more of a statement that warned interlopers that beyond this point was Benito Rojas's kingdom.

On the far side of the wall Bolan made out the long building he had seen from the boat. The area around the building was lit by floodlights on high poles that were bright enough to dispel any shadows. Farther back, maybe a quarter of a mile, was the Rojas house, floodlit as well.

Bolan spent some time checking out the area, covering as much as he could from his restricted position. He was looking for, and found, the armed sentries patrolling the grounds. Some were on their own, and others were in pairs. A couple of teams cruised back and forth in open jeeps, each of which had swivel-mounted 7.62 mm machine guns in place behind the driver.

Every ten minutes a lone sentry moved along the wall, past the Executioner, then turned around and strolled back in the opposite direction. Bolan timed him on two walks. Approximately ten minutes.

He let the man complete his walk, then rolled over the top of the slope and made a run for the cover of the stone wall. Bolan hugged the base of the wall, lowering the heavy items to the grass and freeing his combat knife from its sheath. He waited out the minutes until the sentry came back in his direction. The big American crouched, his back to the wall, and waited as the sentry approached. Once the man passed by, he rose like a black shadow. Leaning across the top of the wall, Bolan caught hold of the back of the guard's shirt collar and dragged him backward across the barrier. The sentry struggled, trying to pull his SMG into play, but Bolan had put a great deal of energy into his move. He pulled the guy over the wall and dropped him facedown on the ground. The man wrestled fiercely, but he was hampered by the hard knee Bolan slammed into his spine. Taking a handful of the Mexican's long dark hair, the Executioner pulled back. The sentry felt a cold sensation as the combat knife cut deep. His throat opened, and the rich flood of his lifeblood emptied itself onto the ground.

Sheathing the knife, Bolan picked up the SMG the sentry had dropped. It was a matte black FN P90, an expensive piece of hardware. As the sentry ceased shuddering, Bolan spotted the compact digital walkie-talkie clipped to his belt. Rojas had equipped his people with up-to-date gear. Bolan was going to have to stay well alert.

Picking up his weapons, the soldier moved quickly. There was no way of him knowing if the sentry had been instructed to call in regularly, or whether a command center contacted him. Either way, the Executioner sensed he was on borrowed time. Vaulting the wall, he checked out the way ahead, then cut off in the direction of the floodlit building, his first port of call.

He flattened against the outside wall, aware of the floodlights casting stark, bright light over the area. A rattle of sound alerted him. Bolan turned, crouching, and saw a side door opening outward. A single figure emerged, SMG dangling from his shoulder. His back was to Bolan as he pushed the door shut.

The Executioner reached up and slid the Beretta from its holster. He brought the pistol on track and hit the sentry with two fast 9 mm slugs through the back of his skull. The guy buckled forward, a burst of bloody spray erupting from his forehead, as he thudded to the ground without a sound. Bolan moved to the door and cracked it open. Peering inside he saw no movement in the dimmed light. He reached down and caught hold of the guard, dragging the limp form through the door. Bolan rolled the body against the inside wall and pulled the door closed.

To Bolan's left a raised three-foot-high concrete walkway looked out across the interior of the building. A quick glance showed him an extensive collection of vehicles. At the end of the walkway, about thirty feet away, was a glass-fronted control room. Bolan could see people inside, their backs turned as they checked out some operation. The Executioner broke into a fast run and headed directly for the control-room door. The thought crossed his mind that the men were trying to raise the sentry he had taken down. He didn't dwell on the thought, just powered ahead, still holding the 93-R.

Bolan was ten feet from the access door when one of the men turned, reaching for a wall-mounted phone. The man's gaze fell on the black-clad, heavily armed intruder running toward the control room. The guy yelled a warning and clawed at his holstered pistol.

Bolan came to a dead stop. Tracking in with the Beretta, he thumbed the selector switch to 3-round burst and triggered the 93-R. The trio of 9 mm slugs smashed through the glass, one of them staying on target and hitting the would-be shooter in the left shoulder.

What the hell, Bolan thought. The time for discretion was over.

The soldier triggered a pair of bursts at the other two men as they turned to face him. He put one down in a flurry of spraying blood. The third guy ducked to one side, placing himself directly in line with the control-room door. Seconds later Bolan hit the door head-on, slamming it open. It hit the guy inside and sent him stumbling backward. As the man tried to regain his balance, the Executioner dropped him with a 3-round burst, then spun and targeted the first guy he had winged. The Mexican, ignoring his bloody shoulder, clawed for his pistol when Bolan shattered his skull with another triburst.

The Executioner took a breath, replaced his partially used magazine for a fresh one and took a long look around the control room. There were TV monitors relaying pictures from cameras placed around the area, a number of telephones on a desk and a rack of SMGs.

Bolan scanned the monitors. They covered the house from different angles on four cameras, the image panning from left to right, then back again. One showed the landing strip and the BBJ2 Boeing Business Jet on the concrete apron. Even in the glare of the powerful floodlights Bolan could make out the jet's cream and blue colors. The size of the aircraft reminded him of the one he had seen coming in for a landing earlier. He was about to turn away when something about the aircraft drew his attention, and he decided to take a closer look to satisfy his curiosity.

Bolan studied the control layout. He had a good grasp of the Spanish language and was able to find out which switches controlled the lights. He managed to kill some of the site spotlights, watching monitor screens go dark as the illumination was cut.

But he had no more time to complete his actions.

Raised voices reached him through the shattered window of the control room. Bolan snatched up the SMG he had put aside and moved away from the exposed window area. As he dropped into a crouch, automatic fire sent a volley of shots into the room, the slugs slamming into the rear wall, blowing chunks from the plaster. A second burst hit the door, penetrating the wood panels and filling the air with splinters. Bolan realized the shooters had to be on the concrete walkway, which left them vulnerable. Staying low, he edged the door open and slid his own SMG around the edge of the frame. As the door swung wide, Bolan spotted the crouching forms of three sentries moving along the walkways. He stroked the trigger of the SMG and sent a long, searching volley in the direction of the trio.

The hail of slugs tore through flesh and bone, kicking the men off their feet. Bolan kept firing, the SMG's muzzle cutting back and forth as it delivered its hot load. The lead man took a substantial number of slugs, half-rising as the pain kicked in. He misstepped and tumbled off the edge of the walkway, his body curving as he fell. He landed hard, blood fanning out across the concrete floor.

His companions, caught in the stream of slugs from Bolan's weapon, had nowhere to go. Jerking and twisting, they spilled their blood on the walkway as they fell, and the Executioner maintained his steady fire until the SMG clicked empty. He threw it aside and slid the Uzi into his hands. On his feet, Bolan moved to the short flight of steps leading to the floor of the building.

29

Bolan looked out across the large garage housing Rojas's fleet of vehicles. It was impressive—cars, SUVs and a collection of panel trucks and tractor units. Quite a setup, Bolan thought, and very useful for ferrying around drug cargoes. He moved to the front of the facility, peered through the side-door window and checked out the dock. He counted a half-dozen powerful speedboats moored there, and saw a number of gunners converging on the building he was in. More of Rojas's security detail. One of the jeeps swung into view, close to the front of the building. The vehicle jerked to a stop, the guy behind the 7.62 mm machine gun swinging the weapon to cover the main roll-up door.

Bolan eased the catch on the side door, yanked it wide and stepped through. The machine gunner yelled a warning, alerting the driver. Bolan's Uzi stuttered, a volley of 9 mm slugs blowing the driver out of his seat and sending the gunner tumbling to the concrete.

Letting the Uzi hang by its strap, Bolan took command of the machine gun as he jumped into the rear of the jeep. He swiveled the weapon and tracked in on the advancing hardmen. His finger eased back on the trigger and held it there. The gun crackled to life, sending a stream of slugs into the running men. Clothing shredded and flesh burst open as the relentless streams of fire cut into the enemy gunners. Staggering, bleeding, moaning they fell in bloody poses. Any shots they fired were either from jerking fingers, or out of panic.

Out the corner of his eye Bolan saw the second gun-mounted jeep sweep into view around the side of the building. The guy behind the machine gun hadn't known what to expect, but it most certainly wasn't to have a supposedly friendly gun turned on him. Bolan raked the jeep from front to rear, rounds punching into the hood and windshield. The driver jerked back, his chest and head pulverized by the continuous blast of automatic fire, his skull split in a bloody fantail of bone and brains. Shell casings littered the floor of the jeep around Bolan's feet as he hammered the other vehicle, keeping up his relentless rate of fire. His heavy bursts riddled the hapless gunner before the guy had a chance to retaliate. Bloody gouts of flesh and blood erupted from his torso as Bolan brought him down. The driverless jeep swerved aside and drove on for yards before the engine stalled and it rattled to a stop. The Executioner hammered 7.62 mm shells at the lower rear until the riddled gas tank's contents caught a spark and erupted in a boiling surge of flame.

The surviving hardmen had watched the demolition of the jeep, and they began to pull themselves together for a concerted rush for Bolan's vehicle. But the Executioner, not forgetting their presence, swung the barrel of his machine gun back on-line and fed them more 7.62 mm damage. Under the hammerlike fire from his machine gun, men went down hard, bodies bloodied and torn. Bone gleamed in glistening pulped wounds.

Bolan's finger let go of the trigger, and the chatter of the 7.62 mm machine gun ceased. The only sound remaining was the moaning of the wounded. The dead held their peace.

In the Executioner's head the clock was ticking. Though the numbers were falling, he knew without a shadow of a doubt there would be other hardmen, such as the security force at the house. How long he might hold them back was anyone's guess.

He stepped from the jeep and turned in the direction of the dock, where his demolition began. Stepping along the timber walk, he reached the line of speedboats. Jumping into the first one, he located the signal locker and took out a flare pistol. Bolan loaded it, then stepped back onto the dock. He moved up to the fuel pump, lifted the hose, flipped the lever and walked along the line, dousing each vessel with raw fuel. Then he backtracked, letting raw fuel soak the wooden dock. Finished, he dropped the gushing hose and returned to dry land, where he fired the loaded flare into the fuel pooling on the dock. The flame rose quickly, raced along the dock, then spilled out onto the speedboats.

Bolan sprinted to the garage and unzipped the satchel carrying the magnetic mines. As he stepped back inside, pausing to pick up any indication he was not alone, the dull thump of exploding fuel tanks reached his ears. Glancing back through the side window, he saw the dock and the speedboats fully enveloped in flames.

Bolan moved quickly along the rows of parked vehicles, randomly placing the timed mines to the steel undersides. He had a ten-minute window. He emptied the satchel and dropped it on the floor as he attached the final mine to a row of high-octane fuel drums.

The Executioner made his way back to the communications room, watching for any Rojas reinforcements. Inside he decided to cut the power to everything he could get his hands on.

He could still hear muffled explosions coming from the distant dock. Bolan felt some satisfaction in that.

The faint sound of a voice caught his ear. It was coming from the handset of the phone on the communications desk. Bolan picked it up. Someone was yelling in rapid, agitated Spanish.

Bolan recognized the voice of Benito Rojas.

"ENGLISH ONLY TODAY," Bolan said.

A pause. Then, "Who is this?"

"Don't you remember me, Rojas? From Cooter's Crossing and the late Marshal Dembrow? At this moment I'm the guy who just made sure your insurance premiums are headed skyward."

He placed the phone back on the desk and returned to the exit door along the walkway, turning as he armed one of the LAWs. He launched the missile at the control room, ducking through the door a second before the explosion. Around him all the security lights dimmed, plunging the whole site into near darkness.

Bolan was beyond the perimeter wall when the planted charges detonated. As the multiple explosions ripped through the garage, destroying Rojas's fleet, the fuel drums blew as well, and a raging fireball swelled through the shredded roof, throwing flame and smoke into the night sky. The rumble of the blasts rolled out like heavy thunder.

Death and destruction, Executioner-style, had just visited Rojas's world, and it was not over yet.

BOLAN SLIPPED his cell phone from its pocket and selected a speed-dial number. He thumbed the button, heard the click as the signal connected, then picked up the ring tone. He waited.

"*Da?*"

"Valentine, I think you've been expecting my call."

"*Tovarich,* where are you?"

"Mexico."

"Is the hospitality as good as it is told?"

"Let's say it's hotter than I anticipated."

"And are you safe?" Seminov asked.

"For the moment. Time for a fast question. Does Bondarchik own an aircraft? One capable of flying as far as Mexico?"

Seminov didn't even have to think before he answered. "During our investigations into anything relating to him, we assessed his properties and ownership of vehicles and such. He owns a Boeing BBJ2 executive jet."

"Cream and blue? With Cyrillic writing on the tail?"

"*Da.* How do you know this?"

"Because it landed here earlier this evening," Bolan said. "Right now it's sitting on Rojas's airstrip. And I'm guessing Vash Bondarchik was the passenger on board."

"My God, I wish I was there with you. But I would settle with Bondarchik once and for all. If you have the chance, say hello to him. Wait, on second thoughts—say goodbye for me."

"Keep your fingers crossed, Valentine. Bondarchik might find it isn't as easy to leave Mexico as it was to enter."

30

Bondarchik's reception was formal. Tomas Trujillo, who seemed to be standing in for his employer, was polite, offering the Russian the best in hospitality. He informed Bondarchik that his flight crew would be brought from the Boeing and given rooms in a guest wing of the house.

Since hearing the news from Danko about the death of Marshal Dembrow and the breakup of the American's organization, Bondarchik had been prepared for a less than enthusiastic greeting from his Mexican client. On that score he was not disappointed. Rojas was not even at the door to his large home when the car rolled to a stop. It seemed it was up to Trujillo to keep the guests entertained. He kept up a stream of lighthearted chatter, and arranged for both men's luggage to be taken to their rooms.

In the open concept living room, stretching the full width of the house, Bondarchik and Litvenko were offered cool drinks to offset the hot evening.

"If you need food, please ask," Trujillo said. "We can offer most anything you would like."

"Two things I would like," Bondarchik said. "One is to see Rojas, and the other is to meet the one chosen to be instructed in the use of the Spyker."

"Hermano Calderon will be here shortly," Trujillo said. "He's looking forward to meeting Señor Litvenko."

Litvenko had already taken one of the offered drinks and found himself somewhere to sit. He never allowed anyone, or any situation to disturb him. He made sure his briefcase stayed close.

Rojas appeared a half hour later, informally dressed and despite his attempts to remain outwardly calm, Bondarchik became quickly aware of the man's mood.

"DO YOU HAVE better news on the shipment?" Rojas asked with little grace.

"When I left Moscow my information was that the ship was on time. It should dock later tomorrow afternoon. In the meantime, Litvenko can take your man through the first stages of the training procedure."

Rojas thought about that, obviously not entirely satisfied, but resigning himself to the facts as they were. He helped himself to a large whisky from the wet bar and drank with the earnest dedication of a thirsty man just returned from the desert. He refilled his glass and beckoned to Bondarchik. They walked through to the open French doors and out onto the wide, stone-flagged patio.

Rojas turned to his guest.

"I should ask your forgiveness, Señor Bondarchik. My recent behavior has been less than polite. My excuse is the sudden turn of events that have quite seriously affected my organization. I am not a patient man. I resent attacks on my authority. But it does not excuse my rudeness to you. I apologize."

"And I accept."

"I am flattered that you came all this way to see me."

"The satisfaction of my clients is important to me. Your disappointment concerned me, so I decided to come speak with you in person to resolve any problems. And my name is Vash. In our businesses, setbacks can be serious." Bondarchik paused before he spoke again. "Forgive me if I touch on delicate matters, but these problems you speak of. Are they to do with the incidents over the border? The last one being the strike against the American Marshal Dembrow?"

"You have heard?" Rojas asked.

"Yes. Tell me, have you learned who is behind these attacks?"

"Only that they seem to have been carried out by a man named Cooper. It is all we have been able to find out. There are no suggestions as to who he works for, though his skills suggest some kind of military background. As far as I can tell, he works alone but seems to have excellent advisory information to direct him."

"From what I understand, U.S. agencies are not allowed to carry out such strategies without sanction."

"The DEA has been trying to build cases against Dembrow and myself for a few years. As you point out, they can do little except make raids on drug consignments and seize the cargo. To actually allow them to step in and make major arrests leading to trials, they need watertight evidence. They have never managed to reach that level."

"So why are they taking such action at this time?"

"A short while ago an undercover DEA agent was discovered within Dembrow's organization. We had him dealt with, and left his body as a statement to the DEA that we would not be intimidated. It is since his death that these incidents started to take place. No information about this man Cooper has been uncovered. He picks his targets and kills without hesitation. He manipulated both Dembrow and myself into trying to regain a stolen cocaine shipment. It resulted in both sides shooting at each other. I will admit he made us look foolish. Despite one of our teams capturing him, he escaped and destroyed a warehouse containing a valuable consignment of hard goods."

"Wearing you down," Bondarchik said. "Creating unrest. Catching you all off guard."

Rojas nodded. "Exactly. And then he went after Dembrow and struck at his house. He destroyed it and blew away Dembrow's security force. Dembrow's organization is gone—there is left. The local authorities have moved in and arrested the few of Dembrow's men left standing."

"Will it affect you?" Bondarchik asked. At the back of his mind was the rest of the money Rojas owed him on delivery of the missile system. "Could the DEA get to you through Dembrow?"

"They might try, but my protection here in Mexico is very good. And legal attempts will be intercepted and challenged. If the DEA makes a fuss, the paperwork will be lost in the system. And the DEA is an American agency. Here in Mexico it has very little authority."

"What about this man Cooper?"

Rojas smiled for the first time, shrugging. "We are ready in case he does step over the border. I have my security around the estate. Let us hope he doesn't make a try while you are here, Vash."

Tomas Trujillo appeared.

"Calderon is here," he said.

"Introduce him to Señor Litvenko," Rojas said. "Find them a quiet place, provide them with whatever food and drink they want and instruct everyone they are not to be disturbed."

The Mexican turned to Bondarchik. "Are you ready to eat now?"

"Yes."

"In the morning we will talk. Tonight we both relax, yes?"

It was the last thing Rojas said before his world exploded.

31

Once Bolan completed his call to Seminov, he edged his way back down the rocky slope to where he had left his M-16, wrapped and hidden. He retrieved the rifle, and made sure he had a full magazine in place and a couple of spares in his pouches. Contrary to his previous decision to leave the weapon behind, Bolan now found he was going to need the longer range for his next move.

The Executioner left his former position and worked his way around the perimeter, keeping a close watch in case any of the Rojas security team swept his current area. With the dock and the garage still ablaze, there was plenty to keep them occupied. Perhaps, Bolan thought, Rojas would have his key people close to the house. He hoped that was the case—Bolan had something else to accomplish before he went after the top man.

Vash Bondarchik's aircraft.

Bolan wanted to disable it, to prevent it taking off. The possibility that Bondarchik himself may have been on board was too good an opportunity to ignore. Stranding the Russian on Mexican soil would be a bonus.

Disabling most of the security lights had left large areas around the estate in total darkness once Bolan moved beyond the burning building and dock. The landing strip was well beyond that area. The big American used the rocky seaward edge of the property to approach the strip. It forced him to a slow pace, but he wasn't concerned. It gave him more time to survey his upcoming target.

Flat on the rocky ground, the water lapping at the shore feet below, Bolan made a thorough recon of the landing strip and the buildings that stood farther back. There was a service hangar, a couple of smaller huts and a control tower. Bolan noted that the strip had its own power supply, because several lights were blazing. One of the smaller huts had to have housed a generator. He also counted at least five armed guards patrolling, and a parked jeep, without a mounted machine gun. Through the glass in the control tower he spotted at least two operators.

As Bolan worked his way farther around the site, he saw a pair of helicopters parked on a circular landing pad. A second jeep stood close by—and this one did have a 7.62 mm machine gun, with an attentive gunner in position.

The focus of attention was the cream and blue Boeing BBJ2. Mobile floodlights ringed the aircraft, spreading a wide oval of intense illumination around the jet.

Bolan spotted a fuel tanker moving away from the aircraft. Bondarchik had obviously made sure the jet was fueled.

Did that suggest he was planning to leave?

Bolan's destructive show of force could have forced his hand. Business aside, Bondarchik would not want to become trapped in the middle of Rojas's enforced war.

Too bad, Vash, Bolan thought. You're here and you can stay.

Bolan was ready to move in closer when he picked up movement to his left. He froze, hidden in the deep shadows beyond the bright lights surrounding the Boeing. Only his eyes moved, picking up the slow-moving, armed sentry easing through the grass edging the landing strip. There was something in the way the guy moved that told Bolan he suspected there was an intruder close by. It showed in his posture, the way he held himself, the muzzle of his SMG tracking back and forth.

The guy was close, now only five to six feet away. Bolan could see he was a big man, broad and solid. Yet he moved with the easy grace of a hunter, his motion fluid, his head moving back and forth, as if he could scent his prey. The Executioner didn't dismiss the thought. Skilled hunters often operated on a level above that of ordinary men. As hunters they survived on their instincts, using every human sense to its utmost. Sound and sight and—yes—smell. Tracking man, the wiliest of prey, required those heightened skills, and this guy, so close to Bolan, was using his.

The Executioner understood, and played the guy at his own game. He made no moves that would attract the hunter. Even the slight rustle of clothing, the merest clash of equipment, could give the prey away. It was all a good hunter needed. So Bolan stayed immobile.

Waiting.

In such proximity to his target, Bolan didn't want to use any weapons that would alert others. He still needed the element of surprise if he was going to carry out his strike on Bondarchik's aircraft. He wanted his attack to be on his terms—not theirs. So he needed that first surprise element to work in his favor.

The guy was getting dangerously close. Bolan caught a sliver of light reflect off his face. Just a sliver but enough to expose the hunter. The guard was almost level with Bolan, eight feet away, still searching. The Executioner knew the situation couldn't last. The hunter's instinct would kick in and he would sense his enemy. When that happened, it would be too late to do anything.

Bolan saw the sentry's head turn in his direction. He observed, almost in slow motion, the dark-skinned, high cheeks, the thick mass of black hair sweeping back as the guy leaned forward. The SMG curved around, seeking Bolan, who moved with surprising speed, considering the weight of ordnance he was carrying. The adrenaline rush added impetus to his leap. The move drove him forward, bodily slamming into the big Mexican. The brute force of the impact pushed Bolan's opponent back, tipping the balance. The soldier jammed a big hand beneath the man's chin, forcing his head back. The move caught the guy off guard. Bolan kept pushing. He heard the Mexican grunt, throw down his SMG. Then he flung both of his muscular arms around Bolan, immediately starting to squeeze. The guy was powerful, his grip bearlike in its intensity. Bolan's feet left the ground and for a moment he was caught in the other man's embrace—this required drastic action.

The Executioner took his hand away from the man's chin, and as the large head lowered Bolan bunched his fist and hammered it into the broad flare of his opponent's nose. He felt the nose break, and the guy grunted against the pain. Bolan hit him again and again, keeping up the brutal assault. Despite the terrible pain and the hot gush of bright blood from his smashed nose, the Mexican kept his grip. Maybe he was hoping his adversary would succumb before the agony of his broken nose became too much to bear. It was a contest of wills between a pair of stubborn and determined fighters. The Mexican shook his head in frustrated rage, blood spraying from his face. Bolan kept up his attack. The guy's nose had lost all resemblance to its former shape. It was nothing more than a crushed and bloody mess.

Sucking in a breath and pushing thoughts of his crushed ribs to the back of his mind, Bolan maintained his physical assault, his pounding fist starting to have an effect on the Mexican's grip. Bolan sensed some relaxation and arched his back, placing his free hand against the Mexican's chest and pushing. The man uttered a low moan and let his adversary drop, as he raised his hands to his bloody face. There was no hesitation in Bolan's actions as he reached down and freed his combat knife. His right hand came up in a calculated sweep that buried the knife deep in the Mexican's chest. Bolan shoved hard, the blade sinking up to the hilt, the keen tip slicing into the guy's pumping heart. Bolan worked the handle, angling the blade so it cut across the heart, enlarging the wound. The Mexican fought the oncoming surge from his dying heart before he toppled with a heavy thud. Panting, Bolan bent over and eased the knife from the man's chest. He wiped it clear and returned it to his sheath.

There was no lingering over his kill. Bolan took a few seconds to suck air back into his lungs, and stretched his body to ease his bruised ribs. He knew he'd be sore later, but that didn't relate to his current situation. He circled the site, bringing himself to where he could get a clear shot at the Boeing.

Down on one knee, Bolan brought the M-16 to his shoulder, using the sling strap to brace his arm. He sighted on his first target, steadied his breathing and fired. The 5.56 mm slug hit true, and the first of the jet's landing wheel tires blew with a soft thump. Bolan adjusted for a second shot. Another hit. Over the next long seconds Bolan methodically blew out every tire on the Boeing's landing gear, watching the aircraft dip and sink a few inches as the burst rubber let the wheels drop to the concrete. He changed position after each few shots, making his exposure difficult.

The Executioner had already fired three shots before the men in the jeep reacted. Their first priority appeared to be for their own protection as both men dived for cover behind their vehicle. Sporadic fire sent bullets winging into the darkness beyond the glare of the floodlights. The slugs were wide. The shooters had no idea where their target was.

As he blew out the final nose wheel, Bolan turned his rifle on the bank of floodlights around the Boeing. His steady rate of fire shattered the majority of the lights, leaving the aircraft in shadow.

He could hear voices yelling in excited Spanish.

Shouldering the M-16 Bolan used the darkness around the aircraft to move in closer. It was time for the big fireworks. He circled the Boeing until he was behind the jeep and its two-man crew. They were still under cover, still sending shots into the darkness because there was little else they could do until they had a solid target. Bolan lifted the Uzi and hit the pair with hot bursts that tore into their bodies and punched them to the ground. He moved on, clearing the immediate area, and crouched behind the cover of wooden packing cases.

From his new spot, Bolan had a clear view of the two helicopters on the pad. He pulled another one of the LAWs into position and primed the weapon. He heard the familiar whoosh as the missile launched, streaking through the night. It impacted against the closer chopper, enveloping it in a burst of orange and red fire. The helicopter blew apart, sending debris in all directions. The second aircraft was badly damaged from the flying debris, its fuselage and canopy burned and pockmarked by shredded metal.

The explosion brought an instant response from the airstrip crew. Bolan's firing position was assaulted by a number of volleys of autofire. The wooden packing cases were reduced to matchwood, but Bolan was all clear, having moved the moment he triggered the LAW.

He chose the armed jeep for his next assault; taking out an armed and mobile target made sense. Bolan had used the relentless power of the 7.62 mm machine gun himself, so he was in no rush to find himself in its line of fire.

The jeep had started to roll as Bolan hit it with the third LAW. The vehicle turned into a moving ball of flame as the missile detonated, its front wheels lifting. Broken parts spun across the concrete as the jeep disintegrated. The driver and gunner were swallowed in the conflagration.

Bolan saw two men rushing his position. He threw aside the LAW tube and brought his M-16 back into play. The Executioner stood his ground, triggering a steady stream of slugs from the assault rifle, and saw the two Mexicans drop. Briefly in the clear, Bolan dug in his heels and sprinted for the base of the control tower. He pressed against the lower wall, sliding an HE round for the grenade launcher into place. Ready, he moved around the base of the tower, stepped back a few feet and targeted the glass control room. He triggered the grenade and almost immediately heard the shatter of glass. The blast spewed broken glass from the control room, debris showered down to the ground. A shrieking man was catapulted from the control room, his arms and legs windmilling as he plummeted to the concrete. His clothing was smoldering from the heat of the blast that had thrown him out the window.

From the control tower Bolan ran to the rear of the service hangar. He took out a single gunner who'd spotted him and was running for an intercept. The guy expressed surprise when Bolan, instead of ducking for cover, turned and spent precious seconds tracking in on his already firing opponent. The Mexican had most likely never faced anyone in close combat. He knew how to jam a trigger back and let a magazine expend itself in seconds, but never realized the tendency of full-auto fire to bounce and move around. Bolan leveled the M-16 and hit the guy with a pair of well-placed slugs that took part of his brain out through the large hole in the back of his skull.

Bolan hauled open the rear personnel door of the service hangar and slipped inside. He heard noise from out front. His adversaries would be searching for him outside, not in the building, so before they came to check, Bolan used his depleting armory to inflict more damage to the Rojas base. The hangar was a busy place. Engine parts, machinery and tools, and a haphazard supply of oil drums and aviation fuel were stacked all over the place. Bolan used a pair of his incendiary devices. He pulled the pins and threw the canisters along the oil-marked concrete floor, then backtracked and got out of the hangar before the heat on Rojas became even hotter. As he slipped into the darkness behind the building, Bolan heard the incendiary devices detonate with soft thumps. He saw the intense glare from the igniting thermate and visualized the rising, terrible heat that would soon be generated inside the hangar.

As he worked his way around the hangar and the demolished control tower, Bolan picked out the shape of the fuel tanker that had recently been filling the tanks of Bondarchik's Boeing. Rojas, he decided, wasn't going to be needing that any longer. The soldier readied his last LAW and fired it into the side of the tanker. He had no idea how much liquid fuel was left in the vehicle, but the missile set it off and the fireball was impressively spectacular and had to have been visible from Rojas's house.

Bolan retreated, leaving the landing strip a burning shambles, and started a long, slow advance toward Rojas's final refuge.

32

The distant crackle of automatic fire was the first indication to Vash Bondarchik that things were not as they should be. He turned to find that his host, Rojas, had snatched up an internal phone and was calling his security crew. Bondarchik could not speak Spanish, so he had no idea what the man was saying, but he caught the rising tone in Rojas's voice and knew it was not good news. The Russian reached inside his jacket and closed his fingers around the butt of the .44 Magnum Desert Eagle he always carried. Just feeling the checkered grips added a moment of satisfaction. He glanced at his bodyguards, alerting them to stand by.

"Benito?" he asked as the Mexican slammed the phone back on its cradle.

Rojas threw a scowling glance at his Russian guest, the thin veneer of politeness fading just as quickly as it had been put in place.

"Not now," he snapped, then began to give orders to his house crew. "Get the servants out. I don't want to be tripping over some idiot trying to serve fucking cocktails if we need to defend ourselves."

The man turned and began to bellow orders to the domestic staff. They took no convincing, especially when they saw everyone wielding firearms. There was a general exodus toward the kitchen and the house's rear exit.

Sensing the coming confrontation, Bondarchik crossed the room and pushed open the door to the office where Litvenko was sitting with Rojas's man.

Litvenko raised his head from the laptop screen he was using.

"What is it?"

"It appears Señor Rojas may have an uninvited guest. One he has decidedly bad feelings toward."

"Did we hear gunfire?"

Bondarchik nodded. "Until I learn otherwise, we will remain under Señor Rojas's protection, Karl. So you and Hermano continue your session, okay?"

"Whatever you say," the unflappable Litvenko said. He glanced across at Calderon. "Are you happy to continue?"

The Mexican shrugged. "This is what I am paid for. I am sure the security crew can handle whatever has happened."

Litvenko returned to his work and Bondarchik backed out of the room.

When he saw Rojas again, standing at a sleek, modern executive desk in a corner of the main room, the man was conversing with Trujillo. The way they exchanged words did little to ease Bondarchik's growing apprehension. He also realized there was little he could do. Not being able to understand the language left him out in the cold. Bondarchik didn't enjoy being out of the loop—his life centered around and depended upon himself being the one in control. This situation made him nervous.

DISTANT THOUGH it might have been, the increase in automatic fire reminded everyone in the house that there was a serious attack taking place. The sudden sharp explosions only increased the tension.

Rojas crossed to a window. He could see the bursts of flame rising into the sky. The location was in the area of the building where the drug lord kept his vehicles. The exchanges of gunfire seemed to be somewhere at the far end of the building, near the dock. The rattle of fire began to lessen. Rojas hoped it meant any intruder—and he admitted to himself he thought it was likely the American, Cooper—had been dealt with.

A few minutes later, after failing to reach any of his security people, Rojas's misgivings returned. The night was lit up by a series of brilliant flashes as fireballs rose into the air. Then a series of dull explosions. One of the house crew came to where Rojas stood.

"Boss," he said, his voice fearful as if he was going to be held responsible, "we saw from the roof that all the boats have been set on fire. The dock, too. It is all ablaze."

"Has anyone called in? Has anyone seen anything?" Rojas demanded.

The man shook his head. "Nothing, boss. We are unable to contact anyone."

"It has to be Cooper," Trujillo said. "Only he would be crazy enough to try something like this."

Rojas rounded on him. Seeing Bondarchik standing close by and listening intently, Rojas switched to English.

"Tomas, I think he is doing more than just trying. Look out there. He is destroying my fucking property. We should allow our guest to hear this as he is involved also."

"Maybe I should—"

"No, no, no, Tomas. I believe you have done enough already. Wasn't it you who agreed with Dembrow to send those idiot American hit men after the DEA agent?"

"He was betraying us all."

"And since he was killed, hasn't this Cooper been exacting his own revenge?"

"Maybe he is not on his own. There could be a covert force working with him."

"You are wrong, Tomas. Cooper is on his own. That is why he is so hard to catch. Whoever he is, Cooper is a professional of high standing. He uses more than just his weapons. The man works with his mind. He has turned things back on us, made us do some of the work. He taunts us. Tricks us."

"But he is only a man, Benito. A bullet will kill him."

"Only if you get him in your sights," Bondarchik ventured. "If he's out there as we speak, he'll use the night to his advantage, stay in the shadows and pick off your crew one by one. He won't stay in one place long—his advantage is his mobility. Your people are in groups. They believe that because they are on home ground they are safe, but somehow Cooper will move around them. The man is a soldier."

Trujillo showed his scorn by his expression, then he said, "How do you figure to know all that shit?"

Bondarchik smiled indulgently. "I wasn't always an arms dealer," he said by way of explanation.

Rojas had been listening to the Russian.

"He is right, Tomas. This American understands combat. He uses the darkness as a friend. While our people tramp around making noise, he will sit in some dark spot and shoot them down."

One of the Mexicans called out, "Some of the security lights have gone out."

Rojas moved to the phone that connected directly to the control room in the garage. He began to yell at the men on duty, but no one replied. Then a voice with an American accent came on line.

"English only today."

"Who is this?"

"Don't you remember me, Rojas? From Cooter's Crossing and the late Marshal Dembrow? At this moment, I'm the guy who just made sure your insurance premiums are headed skyward."

Rojas stared at the phone, a dagger wrenching at his gut.

Cooper. The damn gringo was here, he thought. On his estate. Tearing it apart.

Suddenly there was the sound of a low explosion inside the building.

"Hey, all the security lights have gone out now," someone called.

Rojas screamed in pure frustration. He rounded on Trujillo, jabbing a finger at the younger man.

"Take men. Find this bastard. I don't care how. Just find him and kill him before he pulls this place down around our ears. This time, Tomas, you get your hands dirty. No hit teams to do it for you. Find Cooper and end it. It's time to earn your money. Get out of my sight."

THE THOUGHT OF GOING out into the darkness terrified Trujillo. As with most of his breed, he had little spine for this kind of work. He drove around in a big car, wore expensive clothes and gave orders to others to carry out the wet work. But as scared as he was of the situation, he was more frightened of Benito Rojas. There were few men alive who dared stand up against the cartel's top man—Trujillo was not one of them.

He had just brought his men together, and they were checking and loading their weapons when the entire garage structure exploded in a huge blast that rocked the house. It cracked windows, split plaster and sent pictures sliding from their hooks to crash on the floor. The glare from the blast lit up the area. Debris was hurled for hundreds of feet.

One of Trujillo's team glanced up at the shimmering fireball, shaking his head.

"El diablo anda esta noche," he muttered.

Trujillo was not a superstitious man, but he silently agreed with the sentiment.

This truly was the Devil's night.

33

"We cannot find him," one of the crew called over a handset.

"He is out there somewhere," Rojas shouted.

Bondarchik had his Desert Eagle in his hand, aware that sometime in the past twenty minutes, Rojas had started to lose his control. It might not have been apparent to the Mexican's own people, but Bondarchik had been standing back, observing Rojas closely. The man was sweating badly, his actions becoming more frantic with each passing minute.

The Russian was regretting his decision to make this trip. His idea had been to reassure his client and pave the way for future business. The way things were going, Rojas wouldn't be in the market for any further shipments.

Bondarchik made a fast decision. He moved to an unoccupied part of the noisy room, took out his cell phone and keyed in a number. It connected him to Danko.

"Vash? What's wrong? What is going on there? I can hear shouting."

"Rojas's place is under attack. Half his property has been destroyed. Everything is blown up and on fire. My God, Tibor, it's like being under siege. No, actually we *are* under siege."

"Are you all right?"

"A debatable question. If I could get to the plane, I would take off and get the hell out of here. But this damned American,

Cooper, is suspected of being behind all this. One man and he has Rojas's crew running around helpless. No one can locate him."

"What are you going to do?"

"I'll survive. You are going to get in touch with the tanker and reroute it. Have the captain turn around and get back to Maracaibo. This damned sale is not going ahead, and I am not going to lose that cargo."

"I can't believe this is happening, Vash."

"Swap places with me, Tibor, and you will be convinced."

The conversation was interrupted by another violent explosion that was heard by Danko.

"Something blew up," Bondarchik said, and he was unable to dispel the sensation of dread creeping over him. "Tibor, I have a feeling it might be the airstrip. This American is cutting off every avenue of escape."

Bondarchik heard Rojas in a rapid exchange over the com set he was clutching. He strode over to the man and demanded to know what was going on. When Rojas turned to face him, the Russian felt a chill when he saw the crooked smile on the man's face.

"We may have to extend your stay, Señor Bondarchik. My man tells me the airstrip has been hit."

"My plane? Has he damaged my plane?"

Over the cell Danko was shouting to be heard. Bondarchik ignored it, the cell phone dangling from the hand at his side.

"They can't tell," Rojas said, "and I don't give a fuck. If you want to find out, go and take a look yourself. Be my guest."

"Maybe I should," Bondarchik responded. "I can't do any worse than your sniveling crew."

Rojas dismissed him with a wave of his hand, his attention back on the com set. He had located Trujillo and was screaming orders at the man.

Bondarchik pushed open the door to the room where Litvenko was hard at work.

"Karl, it's time to get out of here. I am going to find out if we still have the means to fly." He realized he still clutched the cell phone, Danko's voice demanding a response. "We are leaving, Tibor. I need to check the plane. I will call you back." He ended the call and dropped the cell phone in his pocket, jammed the Desert Eagle back into its holster.

Calderon glanced at Bondarchik. "That suggests it may be time to move on myself."

"You may be right. Come on, Karl."

Litvenko closed his laptop and followed his employer out of the room.

Bondarchik guided him away from the front of the house, where all the activity seemed to be taking place. The pair of bodyguards, weapons out now, flanked their employer.

"Karl, the flight crew were given rooms along that corridor. Go and alert them. Tell them to leave as quietly as possible and find their way to the airstrip. I'm going ahead to see what has happened."

"From what I hear World War III is what has happened."

"Cheer up, Karl. We will laugh at this over a vodka back home. When you get the crew out, find transport and drive to the airstrip immediately."

Bondarchik turned and made his way through the rear of the house, surprised that there was little activity there. Did Rojas believe Cooper was only going to attack from the front of the property? He didn't question the lack of logic, simply used the situation to his own advantage. He found a door that led outside. Keeping to the shadows, he moved around the house, realizing just how large it was. It took him some time before he cleared the property and used the planted shrubbery and flower beds to conceal his movement.

He emerged on a concrete strip and saw a number of vehicles parked in a neat row. He checked the first one, a heavy American SUV, and opened the driver's door. His bodyguards crowded into the rear. He started the powerful engine and swung the wheel to drive away from the house, following the route that had brought him there originally.

The road curved around in a gentle sweep, dropping down a long slope, and for the first time Bondarchik was able to see the extent of the damage. The dock was ablaze, the gutted shells of burned-out speedboats half submerged in the water. The high flames from the large building just short of the dock had turned night into day. As Bondarchik drove by, he saw the bodies spread around the area. Skirting the section, he angled the SUV in the direction of the airstrip. Fire was still raging, and occasional, smaller explosions added to the scene of carnage. The Russian's sense of foreboding grew as he cleared the last curve and drove onto the narrow road that led directly to the airstrip.

The service hangar and the control tower were demolished, still burning fiercely. Wreckage and bodies littered the scene.

But the Boeing was still there.

Untouched.

Bondarchik drove in the direction of the plane, his means of escape from this mad place. He would take his people, and they would leave Rojas to his struggle against Cooper. The Russian even found the energy to smile as he drew closer to the Boeing.

The expression froze on his lips when he realized the aircraft was not standing squarely. He jammed on the brakes and the SUV came to a shuddering halt. Bondarchik almost fell out of the vehicle in his rush. He stumbled across the concrete, staring in disbelief.

Every one of the Boeing's landing wheels had flat tires. He saw the ragged holes in some of them where bullets had been fired into the rubber. His plane was crippled—there was no way it would get off the ground until the tires had been replaced.

Bondarchik turned. Anger replaced reason, as he tore open his jacket and dragged out the big pistol.

"Cooper. Cooper, you son of a bitch. Show yourself. Let me see you so I can fucking kill you."

34

Bolan had shrugged off as much surplus equipment as possible so he could move faster. He left the M-16 propped against the side of a building but kept the Uzi. He still had his handguns and the combat knife, and decided that was enough for what he had to do.

Crouching in the shadows of high bushes, he watched the erratic movements of Rojas's men as they searched for him. He heard their raised voices—some angry, others tinged with frustration. Bolan's black-clad figure hugged the darkness—his darkened face and hands merged him into near invisibility. The night and Bolan became allies. He allowed Rojas's men to come to him, silently watching their progress. Some had managed to get hold of powerful flashlights, and the wavering beams of light made them easy targets for Bolan's 93-R. Using the foregrip to steady his aim, Bolan waited for a target to wander into range before triggering a subsonic round. There was little sound. More noise came from the impact of the 9 mm slug as it cored into a targeted skull. Bolan put down three of Rojas's men without any of the others even noting their numbers were being depleted. After each shot Bolan changed position, a whispering figure moving around the grounds with deadly purpose, lowering the odds as he brought himself closer to Rojas's refuge.

A nearby shout alerted Bolan. He turned and saw three

gunners rushing in his direction. The bobbing beams of flashlights caught him. Someone yelled orders in Spanish, and Bolan realized that the men carrying the lights had raised the alarm too soon. Keeping the Executioner in their light beams left them fumbling for their weapons—their mistake, Bolan's slim chance. He took it. The Beretta swept on track, Bolan selecting and firing, his single shots digging bloody holes in the hardmen. He put the first guy down with two fast shots to the chest, then dropped and rolled, coming up on one knee to take down the second. The Mexican took a single round to the throat, falling, and the soldier hit him again before the man struck the earth. A hard shot rang out, and Bolan felt a solid thump in his right side, just below his ribs. The impact stalled him for a millisecond before he pumped three 9 mm slugs into the shooter. The guy went down with a high wail. Pushing back the dull ache in his side, the Executioner closed in on the downed men and delivered single shots to the heads to ensure they weren't going to sit up and try again.

He jammed the 93-R into its holster and brought the Uzi into play, moving away from the area and ducking into cover behind a small outbuilding. He crouched in the darkness, his fingers probing the bullet wound. They became moist with blood. He could feel the point of entry and probed deeper. He couldn't be sure how deep the bullet had gone, but at least it wasn't bleeding too much yet.

Bolan considered his position. He was closer to the house now, but on two points his data was zero; he had no idea how many guns Rojas had inside the house, nor did he have a count of the number tracking him through the grounds. On top of that he had just sustained a wound. But the Executioner didn't let that dissuade him. He was committed to his mission, and he would see it through regardless.

He moved on, his target the distant bulk of the house, its lights shining through the wide windows. The place had to have its own generator. There were security lights around the house, some throwing strong light on the frontage, more beamed to illuminate the approach.

Bolan leaned against the trunk of a tree and studied the house.

He could make out people moving about inside. A sudden surge of pain blossomed around his wound. Bolan sucked in a breath and chose to ignore his body's demand that he sit down and rest.

Light caught his attention. The diffused illumination came from a building close by. The security lights around the structure were blacked out, but lights were coming from inside the building, which Bolan noticed was isolated and entirely out of character to the other buildings he had seen.

The wooden structure was long, narrow, with a timber loading bay at one end, and it looked aged. Bolan's curiosity was aroused. If it held anything of value to Rojas, it went on Bolan's list of targets. He stayed in the shadows as he moved its length, searching for an entrance. He found a door and eased it open. It swung on well-oiled hinges, which told him the place had a purpose. Fluorescent lights were attached to the overhead beams. Pulling the door shut, Bolan nodded to himself as he looked at the lines of stacked packages of pure cocaine.

Rojas's main supply was waiting to be shipped out. Bolan didn't even try to assess how much the coke would generate on the streets.

"Millions," a voice whispered.

The cold muzzle of a pistol pressed into the flesh of Bolan's neck.

"That was what you were asking yourself. How much is this all worth?"

A hand reached out and took the Uzi from Bolan's hands, dropping it to the floor. The cold ring of steel didn't move from the soldier's flesh.

He recognized the voice from his earlier phone call to Rojas.

It belonged to Pilar Trujillo's brother—Tomas.

"I knew you would come in here," Trujillo crowed. "See, you are not so smart, Cooper. A man like you could not resist checking out this place. So that makes me the smart one. Yes?"

"So smart you let your own sister be gunned down by Dembrow's goons. Must make you proud, Tomas."

"It was her own mistake. She let herself get mixed up with that damned DEA agent. She could have made things difficult for Rojas. I told her to leave things alone, but she had to interfere."

"It took courage to do the right thing. That's something you wouldn't understand."

"I could kill you right here," Trujillo gritted. Bolan felt the gun muzzle tremble. "Do you not believe me?"

"It doesn't matter what I believe. You'll still be a coward hiding behind Benito Rojas's reputation."

"No." The single word was an enraged protest at the slight against his manhood.

The barrel of the pistol shook, drawing back slightly from contact with Bolan's neck. Before Trujillo could control his anger, the Executioner made his move, pivoting on his heel in a right-hand turn, taking him clear of the threatening pistol. His hands reached to push Trujillo's gun hand aside. He heard the weapon discharge and felt the heat of the slug fan his cheek. Then he had the wrist in his grasp, twisting brutally. Trujillo screamed as pain seared his limb. The pistol fell from his nerveless fingers, and Bolan swiftly slammed his right knee into the Mexican's groin. The force pushed Trujillo back against the wall, and Bolan followed up with a hauled-off punch that hammered across his adversary's jaw. The man's head snapped to one side, then reversed as Bolan brought his right hand across in a backhand blow that had blood spurting from slack lips. Trujillo tried to fight back, but he was out of his league against the towering, black-clad man who remembered the beautiful young woman shot to death in his presence because she had stood up against the power of the drug lord. It was the sodden sound of Trujillo's skull rapping against the timber wall that brought the Executioner back. The Mexican's face was a bloody mask. Bolan wrenched the pistol from his hand, caught hold of the guy's shirt and swung him away from the wall. He pushed Trujillo away from him. The Mexican backpedaled until the high wall of cocaine stopped him and he fell limply to the ground.

Bolan retrieved his discarded Uzi and slipped the strap over his shoulder.

"You won't walk out of here," Trujillo said through mashed and bloody lips.

"Neither will you," Bolan said.

The Executioner backed up to the door and reached into his pouch for the last pair of incendiary canisters. He pushed the door open a couple of inches, then pulled the pin on the first canister. He threw it so that it landed on the top of the coke stash. The second canister he lobbed in a short arc that landed squarely in Trujillo's lap.

Bolan had ducked through the door before the first flash of light from the canisters lit the sky. He loped around the far end of the coke warehouse and heard the tail end of Trujillo's scream before the searing, white hot surge of thermate cut it off. The spreading, hungry burn reached out to scorch the timber walls of the building as Bolan rounded the rear structure and saw the big SUV parked with its driver's door still open and the engine running. Bolan reached the vehicle and threw his Uzi on the passenger seat ahead of him.

He slammed the door shut, dropped the vehicle into Drive and floored the gas pedal. The powerful engine roared, and its tires burned against the ground as the SUV picked up speed. Bolan turned and hit the road, cutting directly in the direction of Rojas's house. It was time to introduce himself to the cartel boss and do it in style.

35

Rojas had lost touch with Trujillo. His last contact had been when the man had called to say he had spotted Cooper and was about to corner him. But Trujillo's cell phone had gone dead, and all Rojas could do was stare from his main house window in horror as his cocaine storage facility went up in flames.

"Damn you, Tomas, where the fuck are you? Why have you…"

The words dried in his throat. Rojas had just spotted the black SUV barreling across the road, racing directly toward the house and the very window he was standing near.

"Here. He is here," he screamed at the remaining crew members.

The SUV loomed larger, bouncing as it sped across the lawn fronting the house. The front wheels hit the concrete edging and seemed to soar as it leaped at the window.

Rojas dropped the phone and hurled himself aside as the vehicle hit the window. There was a jangle of noise, the breaking of glass and the timber frame. Stone crashed into the room and the roar of the SUV's engine filled the air. The SUV scattered furniture and men as it swept across the floor. It came to a sudden stop against a stone fireplace, a screaming crew member pinned, his thrashing body drenched with the torrent of blood gushing from his mouth.

Rojas hit the floor, amid a mass of debris, bruised and aching from his fall. He lay dazed, unable to fully understand how it had all happened—how one man could create such chaos. His thought only generated intense rage. This couldn't be allowed to happen. He was Benito Rojas. He was a powerful man who held influential men in the palm of his hand. His fortune from the drugs he sold had made his income more than the gross national product of some small countries. He bought and he sold. He commanded respect. His word was law…yet right now he was crawling on his hands and knees among the wreckage of his own house.

And all because of a man he had not even laid eyes on.

The crackle of automatic fire reached his ears.

Cooper.

Was he still alive?

He had to see the man, to be there when the trigger was pulled and this nightmare ended.

Rojas stumbled to the SUV and pulled open the front passenger door. The vehicle was empty. He looked across the seat and saw that the driver's door hung open too.

In the swirl of dust filling the room, Rojas saw a dark figure moving, a stubby SMG arcing back and forth. Brief muzzle-flashes came from the weapon. His men were yelling and cursing. The SMG kept crackling, spitting out short bursts.

Rojas worked his way around the SUV, tripping over debris, searching for a weapon. His own pistol was gone, having spilled from his fingers when he had fallen, and in the gloom he was unable to find it.

The shooting died for a few seconds, then resumed. Rojas heard a man scream and beg for mercy—but the firing continued. The man made no more sound.

Then a strange silence fell. The SUV's engine had stalled and there was no more gunfire, only the subdued roar of the burning cocaine storehouse. Rojas experienced a moment of despair when he thought of the vast amount of money going up in smoke. For that alone he wanted to skin Cooper alive.

The drug lord stood in his demolished room, staring around

him. His nerves were shredded. Only then did he feel the warm wash of blood down the left side of his face. He reached up and felt a large and ragged tear in his scalp.

"Where are you, Cooper? Let me look at you, gringo. Or are you afraid to show yourself?"

A soft sound behind Rojas made him turn.

The tall, black-clad figure, his face and hands darkened, made Rojas shiver. The big American was coated in dust, his face blood streaked, and Rojas noted with satisfaction that he was showing a glistening patch of blood across his right side. The eyes that looked at him were a startling shade of blue—cold, ice blue that seemed to cut right into Rojas. The intensity of those eyes made the drug lord catch his breath.

"Tell me who you are. Why you have done all this."

"The who doesn't matter," Bolan said. "We both know the reason why. All of you. Dembrow. Trujillo. Malloy. You. Not one of you have a reason to be allowed to stay alive. You poisoned the very air you breathed. You sold misery and death and walked away laughing because the law couldn't stop you."

A little of the old arrogance surfaced.

"That is true. No laws *can* touch us," Rojas replied.

"Lucky for me then. I don't represent the law. And *I* can touch you."

Bolan saw the expression of sheer surprise on Rojas's face as the muzzle of the Uzi rose. As the drug lord dropped to the floor, desperately searching for a gun, the Executioner touched the trigger and put a burst into the man, leaving a bloody corpse on the floor. The last round hammered into Rojas's skull, splitting bone and depositing the man's brains in the dirt and dust.

36

Vash Bondarchik stood looking around at his despondent crew. They were all at a loss for what to do—until Litvenko turned to his boss.

"Okay. We have no plane. No way of getting it repaired. But we have a car. We should take it and leave this damned place, Vash. Drive until we hit a town and find a hotel. Then make contact with Tibor so he can make arrangements to fly us home."

Bondarchik nodded, understanding exactly what had been said.

"You are right, Karl. Let's do that. Get out of this miserable place before…"

The others were already scrambling to get inside the commandeered limousine. Litvenko had the driver's door opened when he realized Bondarchik had not moved.

"Vash?"

"It's him," Bondarchik said.

"What?"

"The American. Cooper."

Litvenko followed his pointing finger. He saw a tall figure moving slowly in their direction, flame from the still-burning service-hangar illuminating him.

"Let it go, Vash. He came for Rojas. Not for us."

"We would have been gone by now if he hadn't disabled the plane," Bondarchik said.

"So let's go."

Litvenko saw the Desert Eagle in Bondarchik's hand as he walked to face the approaching figure, his armed bodyguards on either side.

"He wanted to keep us here," Bondarchik said. "Why?"

"I don't think he's in the mood to explain, Vash."

"Then I'll make him."

He raised the large pistol.

"Cooper? What is this all about?" he asked, making a sweeping gesture in the direction of the Boeing. "You made me stay. I want to know why."

"A favor for an old friend," Bolan said.

"Friend? What old friend?"

"Commander Valentine Seminov. OCD."

"Seminov? That bastard cop. I should have taken the advice someone gave me recently and had him dealt with. He doesn't approve of me or my business. He thinks I am a mass murderer."

"I have to agree with him on that. You trade in death. Make a profit from it."

"Save me from bleeding hearts. So what did he want you to do?"

"Say goodbye."

Bolan raised the M-16 he had retrieved on his way to the airstrip. Before Bondarchik could get off a shot, he fired twice, the 5.56 mm slugs tearing into the Russian's heart, dropping him dead on the concrete.

Bondarchik's bodyguards were frozen as they saw their boss go down, but they recovered quickly, readying their weapons.

The Executioner had dropped to the concrete, the M-16 tracking, and he opened fire from his prone position. The combat rifle crackled as he continued pulling the trigger. The 5.56 mm slugs blew holes in the bodyguards' expensive suits, puncturing flesh as they cored in, toppling the bulky men to the ground.

Bolan climbed to his feet, slowly, aware of his side wound starting to bleed again.

The muzzle of the M-16 tracked around and settled on Litvenko.

"Weren't you just leaving?" Bolan asked.

Litvenko raised his empty hands. "Yes."

"Do it."

Bolan watched the limo roll away. He fished out the com set and made contact with Casper.

"Come and pick me up, Bud. The airstrip beyond the dock. Bondarchik's aircraft."

"Any resistance still around?"

"I think we probably have the place to ourselves. The last gunners I saw were headed out of here. But bring your protection just in case."

"Hey, you okay, Striker? You sound odd."

"It's been a busy night," Bolan stated.

"Yeah? I can see the lights from here."

"I figured you'd need a guide in," Bolan said.

"Give me half an hour."

The Executioner crossed to the Boeing and made his way up the mobile steps that were still in place. He released the door and stepped inside. The sheer luxury of the interior was overwhelming. Bolan located the kitchen area and searched until he located a first-aid kit. It held enough medical goods to have tended a small army. Bolan stripped to the waist and did what he could to clean up the wound before he applied a makeshift dressing. He eased back into his blacksuit and took a quick look around the kitchen. The well-stocked bar provided him with a bottle of expensive malt whisky. Bolan filled a glass halfway and took a swallow. Maybe not the advised medicine, but right then he didn't give a damn.

Checking out the aircraft he came across what looked like a fully equipped office, complete with a cutting edge computer system. Bolan sat in the big executive chair and switched on the computer. Staring at the Cyrillic script on the large screen, a thought occurred. Bolan used his sat phone to contact Stony Man Farm. He asked for and got Kurtzman and told the man what he had found.

"This looks like Bondarchik's mobile system. You think it could be linked to his mainframe back in Moscow?"

"Only one way to find out," Kurtzman rumbled. "Let me in and we'll suck it dry. Now I'll tell you what you need to do to give me access. Don't worry."

Bolan drained his glass of whisky. The warm glow the liquor created felt good.

"Go ahead, Bear, I'm listening."

Epilogue

From his room in the clinic, Bolan learned a great deal from the news channels on the wide TV screen. There was much speculation over the incidents surrounding the demise of the Rojas Cartel. No one knew exactly what had happened or who was responsible. The story being put out hinted at a major fall-out between the two factions, but the debate continued almost a week after the events. There was plenty of video footage, endless discussions with media faces interviewing representatives from various agencies, and general confusion and speculation. As usual with these things, everyone had an opinion, made up or otherwise.

Bolan didn't give a damn one way or the other. It was over. The agencies could pick over the bones and claim what they wanted. Rojas and Dembrow were dead. So was Bondarchik. Small victories in the big war, but victories nonetheless. Enough for the Executioner.

He was still in recovery. The bullet had been removed, but there had been some infection that left him weak. Bolan took the doctor's advice and gave himself time out to rest. To be truthful, he was glad of the break. Though an enforced one, it was welcome.

His room overlooked the cultivated grounds—smooth lawns and tended flower beds, a world away from the noise of battle.

The crash of gunfire and explosions. Blood and death. The treacherous evil of the enemies he had to face.

And the unwelcome deaths of Don Manners and the beautiful Pilar Trujillo. A twist of fate had brought them together in the wrong place and time. Bolan still carried a little guilt where Pilar was concerned. His intervention had saved her from being hurt at the beginning of their short relationship, but even the presence of the Executioner had not been enough to keep her alive. He would remember Pilar for a long time.

On the positive side there had been bonuses. Kurtzman's cyber magic had reached out and captured the data buried deep in Bondarchik's computer system. His team had unraveled the complicated encryptions and hidden files, opening up a vast treasure trove of information, names, locations. The Bondarchik organization was exposed fully, and once Stony Man Farm had sent the collated data to Valentine Seminov, the OCD had the knowledge and the means to rip the arms dealer's empire to shreds.

Seminov had been wild with excitement when he called Bolan at the clinic and told him of the success the OCD had achieved.

"They were like rats jumping a sinking ship, *tovarich,*" he said. "We had so much evidence it was overwhelming. The lawyers suddenly backed away and began to deny any connection to Bondarchik. It was wonderful to watch. Even Tibor Danko had nothing to say when we arrested him. Bondarchik's contacts in high places started to blame one another. It will take months to sort it all out. Cooper, I owe you so much for this. I will always be in your debt. For everything. Not forgetting that you delivered my last message to Bondarchik in person."

"One less to worry about," Bolan said.

Brognola was happy with the outcome, and so was the President. Because of his need to stay distanced from the mission, he had not been able to speak to Bolan in person. His thanks were passed along via Brognola, who made it clear the Man felt deeply obligated to Bolan for what he had done and the risks he had taken.

"You have a fan there," Brognola said. "Coming through the way you did has made him realize there are still individuals who give their word and see it through. He won't forget in a hurry.

"By the way, Aaron found out the name of that oil tanker. A Navy ship located her, turned her around and she's currently headed back across the Gulf. The captain took a chance and put a search party on board. They found the missile launchers in one of the tanks. They had been broken down into parts and packed into sealed containers submerged in crude oil. They found some conventional weapons, too. The tanker was escorted to an American naval base. The oil tanker's captain has some explaining to do. He could be in custody for some time."

"Let's hope he likes Navy food."

"The DEA has been dogging Eugene Corey on his association with the Rojas-Dembrow Cartel. It helped when I slipped them evidence of telephone calls he'd made to Quinn and those cash payments we traced to Chris Malloy. Added to Don Manners's data, they're going to get some hard results."

"Hal, what about the Mexicans forced to work for Dembrow?"

Brognola's smiling face had filled the sat phone's screen. "All being worked out through Customs and Immigration. Justice put in a good word and so did the DEA. And that suggestion you offered about channeling that cash you liberated from the hit team to assist them is going to help. Don't look at me like that. I'm on top of it. I'll see it gets into the right hands."

Bolan knew he could trust his old friend.

The soldier would stay in the clinic just for as long as it took Jack Grimaldi to get there, then he'd get his old friend to head north for a little R and R. He'd spend a few days at the Farm.

It was time to heal.

But Bolan knew another mission would soon appear on the horizon. One always did.

* * * * *

JAMES AXLER

DEATH LANDS®

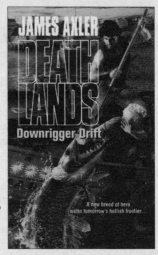

Downrigger Drift

A new breed of hero walks tomorrow's hellish frontier...

In the nuke-altered region of the Great Lakes, Ryan and his group face the spectrum—from the idyllic to the horrific—of a world reborn. Against the battered shoreline of Lake Michigan, an encounter with an old friend leads to a battle to save Milwaukee from a force of deadly mutant interlopers—and to liberate one of their own.

Available January 2011 wherever books are sold.

GOLD EAGLE®

www.readgoldeagle.blogspot.com

GDL96

AleX Archer
RESTLESS SOUL

The relics of the dead are irresistible to the living...

A vacation spot picked at random, Thailand ought to provide relaxation time for globe-trotting archaeologist Annja Creed. Yet the irresistible pull of the country's legendary Spirit Cave lures Annja and her companions deep within a network of underground chambers— nearly to their deaths.

Available January 2011 wherever books are sold.

GOLD EAGLE®

www.readgoldeagle.blogspot.com

GRA28